Let Michael R. Perry Be
Smart, Practical Wedding Talk
That Will Keep You Laughing, Too!

The Couple's Wedding Survival Manual

A savvy guide to planning your wedding, this is the one book you'll both turn to for answers and advice on

- picking a place for your wedding—from a church or synagogue to a less traditional venue

- ground rules for discussion: how to keep a lively debate on the virtues of a five-piece band from becoming a flare-up about money, family, etc.

- choosing your invitations—and choosing them again after a fight (repeat as often as necessary)

- realistic spending—and the myth that expensive weddings ensure happy marriages

- having the wedding you really want, while remaining on speaking terms with your family members when it's all said and done.

Books by Michael Perry

The Couple's Complete Wedding Survival Manual
The Groom's Survival Manual

Available from Pocket Books

For orders other than by individual consumers, Pocket Books grants a discount on the purchase of **10 or more** copies of single titles for special markets or premium use. For further details, please write to the Vice-President of Special Markets, Pocket Books, 1633 Broadway, New York, NY 10019-6785, 8th Floor.

For information on how individual consumers can place orders, please write to Mail Order Department, Simon & Schuster Inc., 200 Old Tappan Road, Old Tappan, NJ 07675.

The Couple's Wedding Survival Manual

How to Tie the Knot Without Coming Unraveled

Michael R. Perry

POCKET BOOKS

New York London Toronto Sydney Tokyo Singapore

7746134

The sale of this book without its cover is unauthorized. If you purchased this book without a cover, you should be aware that it was reported to the publisher as "unsold and destroyed." Neither the author nor the publisher has received payment for the sale of this "stripped book."

An *Original* Publication of POCKET BOOKS

 POCKET BOOKS, a division of Simon & Schuster Inc.
1230 Avenue of the Americas, New York, NY 10020

Copyright © 1999 by Michael Perry

All rights reserved, including the right to reproduce this book or portions thereof in any form whatsoever. For information address Pocket Books, 1230 Avenue of the Americas, New York 10020

ISBN: 0-671-53790-3

First Pocket Books trade paperback printing January 1999

10 9 8 7 6 5 4 3 2 1

POCKET and colophon are registered trademarks of Simon & Schuster Inc.

Book design by Alma Orenstein
Cover design by Jeanne M. Lee

Printed in the U.S.A.

Contents

Chapter 1

We're in Love!
We're Engaged!

(Now What Do We Do?)

AMERICAN STOCK PHOTOGRAPHY

*W*as it love at first sight? Or was it one of those delicious slow-building romances where each of you secretly kept an eye on the other, wondering if the feeling was mutual, until the day you both realized that it was foolish to wait any longer? However it happened, you fell in love with each other, and nothing will ever be the same. Suddenly, it all makes sense: *that's* why we're here. *That's* what all those people are singing about. No longer content merely to clock time here on planet Earth, the two of you discovered each other, and it's starting to seem like things happen for a reason.

Then, you got engaged, and perhaps that was the most romantic moment of your life so far. You made a promise that some time in the near future you'll exchange vows and make permanent the best thing that's happened to either of you. It's a simple decision with profound implications for both of you. There's a new constant in your lives: no matter what happens, you'll be there for each other. You'll celebrate the good times together and you'll shore each other up during the not-so-good times; you'll witness the marvels of the new millennium with someone you love; and *from this day forward until the end of time,* you'll be able take full advantage of every one of those buy-one, get-one-free offers ("at participating locations"). Yes, marriage is a wonderful thing.

Planning the Wedding: A Preview of Your Life Together

After falling in love and getting engaged, there's just one remaining obstacle before marriage—the wedding. Before diving into the next couple of hundred pages explaining the occasionally obsessive minutiae of wedding planning (e.g., half-leaded crystal or fully leaded crystal—page 6) take a moment to understand the important distinction between your *wedding* and your *marriage*. Your *marriage* should ideally last many, many years, during which the two of you will grow older, wiser, and closer together. Much if not most of what will happen cannot be predicted, and it's an article of faith that whatever comes your way the two of you will face together.

Your *wedding,* on the other hand, will last one day. Even including the dinners, showers, and receptions surrounding a big wedding, we're talking *maybe* a couple of weeks, max. (Unless you're a crowned head of state, in which case you don't really need this book, do you? Just go ask the royal advisors for help.) This book is designed to help both of you make the time spent planning your wedding as memorable and enjoyable as possible. It's meant to help you learn wedding traditions, old and new, so that you may choose those elements you wish to include and ignore or modify those you don't.

This book is also meant to help both of you keep the wedding in proper perspective. No matter how lavish or "perfect" a wedding appears, it will be a failure if the bride and groom have become estranged from each other. A certain level of spirited argument is a fine thing, but at the end of every day during this period you should kiss and make up. Many unnecessary fights are fought by couples striving to create an unrealistically fancy wedding based on something they saw on television or read in a book.

The time spent planning a wedding together is a good trial run for your marriage. When unexpected problems arise, you'll solve them together. You'll have moments when you disagree on which direction to take or which choice to make about the wedding, but you can learn how to negotiate and compromise to arrive at a decision satisfactory to both of you. Planning a wedding, you'll run a gauntlet that sets the two of you against challenges in a variety of fields—families, friends, the law, religion, money—and you'll use virtually every important life skill that can't be taught in schools.

The Art of Negotiation: Getting Married Without Breaking Up

Before you bought this book, chances are you discussed some of the decisions ahead of you. Maybe you even disagreed. Perhaps one of you wanted a big wedding and the other wanted a small one. Maybe there was a debate (not an argument! It wasn't an argument!) about where to hold the wedding: his town or hers? Church or courthouse? Religious, civil, or both? If so, you are the first couple ever in the history of mankind to have disagreements while planning a wedding. It has never happened before; all the people you know who are married were in perfect harmony about every choice and their families and friends backed them 110 percent, never pressuring them or advancing their own agendas.

Okay, that's not entirely true. *Some* couples may have had *one* or *two* disagreements along the way. There was this couple over in Iowa who had *three* disagreements, but let's not talk about them.

Just kidding. Disagreements are what make life interesting. Most couples actually have lots of little disagreements during the planning of a wedding, and even more during their marriage. The surprising thing is the incredible variety of subjects

He did it. He popped the question. Now what?

AMERICAN STOCK PHOTOGRAPHY

over which disagreements can arise. For example, three weeks before getting engaged, chances are neither of you knew what engraved printing* was, and now you have to decide whether it's worth paying extra for.

So, how do you handle these disputes? *Negotiation.* As long as you understand in advance that there'll be some disagreements (okay, lots of 'em) and you both promise to fight fair, there's no reason why any single dispute or even a long and tedious series of disagreements should rock the boat. Just agree to some ground rules:

1. *Argue only about the subject you're arguing about.* If you start off in a debate about the relative virtues of a five-piece band versus a disc jockey, it is against the rules to launch into a general discussion about how one of you is a tightwad and the other a spendthrift. Nor is it permissible to switch into a discussion about how if we didn't pay for those &*@! engraved invitations we'd be able to afford the five-piece band.

2. *Promise not to dig in your heels on subjects you don't care about.* This sounds obvious, but at the end of a long day of wedding planning, one or the other of you might feel the need to take a stand on a subject that if you thought about it, you really have no opinion on one way or the other. Engraving, for example.

3. *Remember that either way the decision goes, you both still win.* You can have an all-kazoo orchestra, a minister with hali-

---

*What is engraved printing, you ask? It's an expensive and archaic method of printing invitations (or anything else—U.S. currency is engraved) that uses a custom-made steel or copper plate in an intaglio printing process. Ink sits in the recessed wells of the plate while the printing press exerts force on the paper, pushing it into the wells and onto the ink. Engraving costs more, but snooty people often run a fingertip along an invitation to feel for the telltale ridge that indicates engraving. Absurd? Maybe. Maybe not. That's for *you two* to discuss.

tosis, a reception packed to overflowing with ex-cons and politicians, food from a school cafeteria, and a limo that smells like formaldehyde and at the end of the wedding day, you'll still be married—which is, after all, the goal.

4. *Spend a little time every day talking to each other about something other than the wedding.* Sometimes, you can lose sight of the forest for the trees. Two minutes is all it takes to remind yourself that you still love each other—it's just the wedding that's driving you crazy. If you can't think of something, try one of these: "You look great today!" or "How many food groups are represented on a pizza?" or even "Ever notice how both *Star Trek* captains are bald but only one wears a rug?"

All right then. Now that you know *how* to argue, it's time to get to the subject at hand. You've got about a thousand decisions between "Will you marry me?" and "I do." A little information will help you make the right choices most of the time, and a good attitude will tide you over during the few times you make the wrong ones. Enough self-esteem jibber-jabber and goofy jokes. You have a wedding to plan.

*H*owever it happened, you fell in love and nothing will ever be the same.

AMERICAN STOCK PHOTOGRAPHY

Chapter 2

Your Families, Your Friends, and the Two of You

Whose Wedding Is It, Anyway?

*Y*our wedding will be a public event.

AMERICAN STOCK PHOTOGRAPHY

$\mathcal{T}$he first kiss the two of you shared was yours alone—sweet and unique, your first joint foray into the terra incognita of intimacy, something that belongs to you alone. That moment when you realized it was true love, love worth sustaining for a lifetime, belongs to the two of you as well. No one else can share the magic moment when the two of you became engaged—nor could anyone understand the special feeling you alone shared.

Your wedding . . . will be just a little different. Your wedding will be a *public* event, which differs from those private moments enumerated above. Of course the two of you will be the ones getting married, but you'll also share that special day with the officiant, your parents, your grandparents, the rest of your family, your friends, the people who think they're your friends but really aren't, the governor of the state you live in, the Internal Revenue Service, a caterer named Rafaelo, people you regret inviting, the manic-depressive flower lady, and 41 vendors supplying products and services ranging from preprinted reply cards to edible garters. Isn't it romantic?

Early on—right now is a good time—familiarize yourself with the concept that a wedding is a ceremony for the two of you *and your community.* Even if you plan to tie the knot at the courthouse, invite no one, and never finger a finger sandwich or give a toast, a witness will still be required. The witness represents society. After getting a license from the state where you live (more about that in chapter 8) the two of you will exchange vows in front of at least one witness, and probably quite a few more. So whose wedding is it?

One answer may be that it's *your* wedding, so you should do it the way you see fit and let the rest of the world play catch-up. But the ceremony in a vacuum lacks meaning; you've already agreed in private that you love each other. It's time to test-drive that lifelong commitment under real-world conditions.

Perhaps it helps to prioritize. If you already have a stack of bridal magazines (admit it—you bought several at the same time you bought this book), it's easy to get the impression that a wedding is a shopping spree followed by the most expensive party you've ever thrown. Bridal magazines leave the indelible impression that the amount of money spent is directly proportional to how much you love each other. Without ever spelling it out explicitly, the message comes across in those glossy spreads that if you don't purchase every product advertised therein, then you won't have a good wedding and by extension won't have a good marriage. Well, here're two hints that this might not be entirely true: First, the advertisers in all those mags pay big money to make you think that's the case. Second, if it were true that more stuff equals a better marriage, then a big, expensive wedding should guarantee a terrific marriage. Elizabeth Taylor has spent millions of dollars on weddings—something like eight of them. If there were any relationship between money spent on the wedding and a happy marriage, one wedding would have done the trick, but instead, the streets of America are littered with Elizabeth Taylor's ex-husbands. Now, if her weddings had been smaller, would she (and one of her many ex-husbands) have found happiness? Probably not. But her experience is ample proof that an expensive wedding doesn't ensure a happy marriage.

People who celebrate Christmas are fairly aware of the general sentiment that "commercialization" may have ruined the "true meaning" of the holiday. Annually, commentators on

$\mathscr{D}$arling, we both enjoy semiformal evening attire and filtered menthol cigarettes—what say we tie the knot?"

AMERICAN STOCK PHOTOGRAPHY

the editorial pages of newspapers and at the end of local television newscasts get on their soapboxes and implore everyone to knock off the commercialization and get back to the basics. Well, your wedding is not going to be a national holiday, so Andy Rooney's not going to chide you from his *Sixty Minutes* perch, but remember: your wedding isn't entirely about buying stuff and spending money. Buy as much stuff as you want, but try to remember that while shopping can be lots of fun, it's not the main point.

Families

Once upon a time, marriages were arranged by the families of the bride and groom and the couple actually getting married were among the last to know. In some countries, this is still the case. Arranged marriages had the advantage that both sets of in-laws had come to terms with each other long before the bridesmaid gowns were selected; the disadvantage was only that the two people exchanging vows were forced against their will to marry without any concern over whether they loved each other. Heck, when they arranged marriages, they didn't even have to consider if the people getting married wanted to marry anyone at all. Marriage wasn't something you chose to do; it was something that happened to you, like a bad cold or a broken leg.

Fortunately for the bride and groom, we live in a more enlightened age and adults have earned the right to determine their own marital destiny. Unfortunately, it's now *your* obligation to grapple with your two families. A few weeks of that and you understand why arranged marriages had some small advantages.

With all the different kinds of stepfamilies and blended families and virtual families and every other kind of family out there, it may seem futile to propose a working definition of what a modern family is (though this won't stop Bill Moyers from making a 10-part special on the subject). However, for the purpose of planning for your wedding, *family* could be defined as "all those people who will generously help with your wedding."

Or perhaps a better definition of *family* might be "all those people who want to interfere with your wedding and impose their views."

Wait! They're *exactly the same people!* Your families will simultaneously make your wedding a memorable, meaningful, and enriching experience and drive you nuts. That's the beauty of it, and walking that fine line between "the most important people in my life so far" and "let's get away from these maniacs and elope" requires a little diplomatic finesse. Rest assured that the family skills you develop preparing for your wedding will last you the rest of your life.

The good part needs little explanation. Your families helped make each of you what you are today. They may provide some degree of moral and financial support as you head toward the altar, as well as a sense of tradition and continuity in your life. Some couples like to incorporate family heirlooms into the wedding ceremony, like a grandmother's wedding ring or a father's formalwear. This provides a palpable connection to the past and the sense that your wedding is part of a long tradition.

Your respective families will provide guidance and direction, which is welcome . . . to a point. When her mother helps the two of you select a place to exchange vows, that is welcome assistance; when she feigns a heart attack on learning that you'll do it somewhere other than the exact spot she thinks is right, then she has crossed over into interference.

How do you solicit input from both families while reserving final judgment for yourselves? How do you take advantage of the best your families have to offer without losing your

$\mathscr{Y}$ou may think your families are as different as night and day, but chances are they have *something* in common.

AMERICAN STOCK PHOTOGRAPHY

way in the barrage of "assistance" that rains down on you? The answer may help you throughout your entire marriage, and that is to present a united front to the world. If the two of you want to get married on the pony ride in the city park and you've given it all the thought in the world and decided between yourselves that it's the thing you really want to do, then you need to endure the slings and arrows of those who would second-guess you *together.* If Mom and Dad and Sis and everyone else begin agitating against the pony ceremony, it's important that the two of you stick together. In public. In private, wedding planning (and later, married life) is one never-ending negotiation. Though neither of you wins all the time, each learns that greater satisfaction grows out of fulfilling your spouse's wishes than out of getting your own way all the time.

After the two of you finally agree on a compromise between yourselves, the time comes to grapple with the rest of the world, which, at last count, was up to around 5 billion people, all of whom either want to come to your wedding or have something to sell you that you absolutely, positively must have in your wedding. There may be times when you have to say no to a friend or a relative, even when you generally agree with that friend or relative, just because you and your spouse-to-be agreed on something different. That's hard.

A typical encounter might go like this:

Friend: *So I just need you to tell me at what point in the ceremony I'm supposed to play the accordion concerto. Just say the word and I'm there.*

You: *I don't think we're going to use the accordion concerto after all.*

Friend: *But you said back in college that if you ever got married I could play it—*

You: *My fiancée (fiancé) and I talked about it and decided that*

maybe our wedding just wasn't the right place for Memories of
Lawrence Welk in B Minor. *I still love the accordion and
you're still a good friend—*
Friend: *That's not what it looks like from here.*

And maybe you really do love the accordion, and maybe
you sort of wanted the friend to play that special concerto,
but there just wasn't time in the wedding to do so. With all
the anticipation focused on a wedding, it's easy to overplan; at
some point, the realization dawns that it will be a day with 24
hours like any other, and something will have to go.

Another example: Everyone in *his* family for three genera-
tions has gotten married at the old church on Main Street in
his grandparents' hometown of Hadleyburg. His family's
name is on the cornerstone of the church; his great-uncle
Eustacius posed for the stained-glass window nativity scene
(as the third shepherd from the right.) You could say he's got
roots in Hadleyburg.

But *her* family lives in Metropolis, a good nine-hour drive
from Hadleyburg, and he and she both have lived in
Metropolis a good long time as well, so a Hadleyburg wedding was out of the question. The two of them agreed that
though Hadleyburg and Metropolis both had their attractions,
Metropolis would be the best site for the wedding. Agreed.
Handshake. "That's where we'll have the ceremony." The
end—or is it? Can decisions that were final come back from
the grave like the killer in a *Friday the Thirteenth* movie?
Sometimes the answer is yes.

He might have relatives start second-guessing him: "Mom
and Pop got married in Hadleyburg, and so did Grandma and
Grandpa, and so did their parents before them," he might
hear, "so I guess you really don't love your family." That hurts.
Or, more likely, it might not be the frontal assault but some
sneakier attack, the kind of hot-button pushing that only

𝒴ou said I could play at your wedding."
"Yeah—when we were in the third grade."

AMERICAN STOCK PHOTOGRAPHY

blood relatives can do so well. Before the end of the week he might think that he was stupid to agree to get married anywhere else but Hadleyburg. . . .

Meanwhile, his bride-to-be was out booking churches, reception halls, and brass bands. When he drops the last-minute change-up that he wants to get married in Hadleyburg after all ("It's only a nine-hour drive—seven if you risk your life"), they have a fight on their hands—as they should, because she's already paid deposits on all the places they're going to need, and more important, they already agreed to agree.

Could this confrontation have been avoided? Maybe so, if he had been firm but fair with the relatives, asserting that he still loved the family hometown but had decided to get married elsewhere. Your engagement is a good time to practice an important skill that will make your marriage much happier, and that is this: sticking to "an agreement between the two of us is final." When the two of you hash out something you both can agree on, that's it. Finality. Put the second-guessing out of your mind and proceed as if you had received a decree from the president of the United States. Others will sense your resolve as you carry out your wedding plans with an air of certainty. Soon that confidence will spread to other areas of your lives, and you will open a small business together, which will soon blossom into a large business, and soon we'll all be working for you as you run the world.*

Actually, whether or not you'll be running the world (and if you are running the world, let me recommend myself as ambassador to some pleasant island nation right now), having

---

*My lawyer says I can't make these kinds of promises, so maybe you won't be running the world in a few years, but it could happen. Your mileage may vary. Not available in certain states. Consult your physician before following any specific advice.

iron-clad agreements between the two of you will make life easier. If Mr. Hadleyburg, above, had simply taken the agreement between himself and his fiancée as gospel, the discussions with family members might have been shorter. "Nope. Already decided. Getting married in Metropolis." The end. If they had argued with him, he could have reminded himself of another truth about agreements between spouses: if you can't take the heat from others, be prepared to take it at home. In other words, if he had just endured his family's abuse, he wouldn't have (deservedly) taken it from his fiancée.

Decisions, Decisions

Your family (however you define it) is not the only group of people who have demands on your wedding; so do lots of other people, including friends, the clergy, the caterer, and so on. Time and time again, you'll have to make decisions as to how, when, where, and with whom you will celebrate your wedding. The best choice is to make decisions as a couple, but that isn't always possible. So when dealing with all the other people who have a proprietary interest in your nuptials, how do you keep your wedding your own? *How do you let others become involved without having them overwhelm your plans?*

Read carefully, because this life skill will serve you well long after your wedding. It takes into account people's natural inclination to want to help; it lets others participate in your wedding (and later, your life) in a way that is satisfying to them and helpful to you. In short, we're looking at what those business types call a "win-win" proposition—a situation where you get what you want, they get what they want, and everyone's happier. All this without violating any of the basic laws of physics. It's called—

Participation by delegation.

If people want to help out, give them small tasks they can handle. The way to win favor from others, according to top psychologists, is to let them do favors for you, and not, as you would expect, the other way around. You can genuinely be thoughtful and engaging while having others help you with the myriad details of planning your wedding.

Don't take it on faith. Test out the proposition with a small detail of wedding planning and be amazed at the result. The next time someone calls to give his or her opinion of how your wedding should be, listen carefully, then turn that person loose on a task that can't be screwed up.

"Hello?"

"It's me—Auntie Em."

"Hi. How are you?"

"I was thinking about your wedding. Maybe you should do it in polyester. It lasts forever, you know."

"What do you mean?"

"The dress, the tuxedo, the little things that the flower girls wear—I think they should be polyester."

This is the spot in the conversation where lesser souls feel that they're receiving undue interference from a friend or relative. But you know better. You know how to turn interference into help—

"I don't know if we're going to do that, Auntie. But I do need your help."

"You do?"

"Yes. You know all about flowers, don't you?"

"A little—"

"Well, we want to have irises in our wedding and don't know where to go to get them."

"They're not going to be in season—"

"That's exactly the problem. Do you think you could call a few florists and see if there's any way we can get some irises for the wedding? It would be a big help."

"I'd love to."

In one simple phone call, a meddler was converted into a helper. Auntie Em just wanted to help—meddlers never think they're meddling—and now she has something to do. You needed to know where irises could be obtained out of season, and she's going to feel that she was part of the wedding. In fact, she'll be able to point out the irises to other wedding guests and explain "what an ordeal it was to find irises at this time of year."

You may say, "But I don't have an auntie Em, and wouldn't have irises at my wedding even if you paid me." If that's the case, please sit at the back of the class, because we're illustrating a concept with an example; you don't have to have an auntie Em or irises at your wedding. The challenge is to create things that (1) need doing, (2) don't require enormous judgment or discretion, and (3) will give the doer a real sense of participation. During the months before the wedding, this can include the following:

- A trusted relative can be put to work finding the correct addresses—and the spellings of surnames—of far-flung relatives who will be invited to the wedding.
- A close friend can help you by doing the same for friends who have moved out of town and/or gotten married themselves (names change—but not always).
- Someone who is good with drawing can make maps that show the way to the ceremony and/or reception for out-of-towners or just for people who get lost easily.
- A good calligrapher can be a great help when addressing envelopes—invite him or her over *after* the invita-

$\mathscr{Y}$es, I'm looking for one hundred eighty banana-yellow polyester cumberbunds."

AMERICAN STOCK PHOTOGRAPHY

tion list has been finalized and the invitations have been purchased.

- A business-minded friend or relative can make a few phone calls you just don't want to. For example, if you interviewed several bands and liked them all, let someone else give the bad news to those who didn't make the cut.

No definitive answer can be given to the question Whose wedding is it? In one sense, it's yours alone; but in another important way, it belongs to the community at large. With a little delegation and some careful planning, you can make the wedding unique for the two of you while involving friends and loved ones every step of the way.

Chapter 3

Jewelry

AMERICAN STOCK PHOTOGRAPHY

*M*any if not most couples incorporate three important pieces of jewelry into their nuptials: one engagement ring and two wedding bands. None of these are obligatory, yet for those who choose engagement and wedding rings, they carry a powerful sentimental and symbolic punch.

Jewelry advertisers like to use this symbolism to make you abandon all common sense and blow a big wad of cash to purchase them at the exact time in your life when you might need to shepherd every penny.

A good strategy to prevent yourself from being taken advantage of is to make two lists. The first list enumerates all the reasons why the rings are a terrific, loving gesture. The second lists why they cost so much money. If you compare the lists, you'll find no overlap.

Engagement Rings Are Sweet Because . . .

1. They are a daily, constant reminder to the bride-to-be of the promise that she will be married, soon, for certain, to the man who gave her the ring.
2. Engagement rings are the best conversation starter in the world; for example (excitedly): "Is that an engagement ring?" (Broad smile): "Yes it is." (Long stunned pause from questioner, followed by shrieks of excitement.) It just does not get much better than that.
3. An engagement ring can carry a secret message on its inside rim that is shared only by the two of you—

perhaps with the date of your engagement and your secret pet names: "From Pookie to Pudding, January 22."

4. An engagement ring is a hard and fast sign that your relationship has made the quantum leap from the no-man's-land in the battle of the sexes labeled variously as "just dating" or "just living together" and is now headed for the green pastures of a real, solid commitment.

Having said why engagement rings are *valuable*, let's see why they are so *expensive:*

Engagement Rings Are So Outrageously Priced Because . . .

1. If it's a diamond ring, as many are, it will be expensive because one South African company, De Beers Consolidated Mines Limited, controls almost all the diamonds that are sold in the world. This is called "a monopoly" (not the game) and they keep prices artificially high by ensuring that there are never too many diamonds for sale on the open market at one time.

2. See reason number 1.

Engagement Rings

Despite the cost, many couples still want a diamond engagement ring, a "tradition" that dates back several ad campaigns. If you choose to buy a diamond engagement ring there are many questions you may ask:

Q. *One jeweler in our town advertises that its diamonds are guaranteed to appraise for at least double what we pay for them. How can this be?*

A. By using a fast-and-loose definition of the word *appraise,* you could appraise it for ten times as much as you pay for it. However, if by "appraised at double what you paid for it" jewelers mean someone else will *pay* that much for the gem, why wouldn't they sell it to the person who will pay that much, instead of taking half as much from you?

Q. *Another diamond dealer advertises that its merchandise is offered "wholesale to the public." What does that mean?*

A. Selling to the public means that you are in the retail business. You can call a rabbit a "miniature polar bear with big ears," but that doesn't make it one. "Wholesale to the public" just means "retail that we're pretending is wholesale."

Q. *But our friends bought an engagement ring from that "wholesale to the public" joint and got a really good deal.*

A. Your friends are special people and would never intentionally speak a mistruth, but unless they bought a whole bunch of diamonds at once, they were engaged in a *retail* transaction. To wit, *Merriam Webster's Collegiate Dictionary,* tenth edition, says

retail *n:* the sale of commodities or goods in small quantities to ultimate consumers.
wholesale *n:* the sale of commodities in quantity usu. for resale (as by a retail merchant).

Someone who sells diamonds wholesale gets a phone call from another diamond dealer who might say something along the lines of

"Hey, Jack, I'm making some tennis bracelets and need fifteen or twenty quarter-carat diamonds, not especially good quality. Got anything?"

"Yep. I'll send over twenty and bill you at the end of the month."

"Thanks."

That is a *wholesale* transaction. Painless and quick, and the guy who's doing the buying takes responsibility for knowing what he's getting.

A *retail* transaction consists of a couple wandering in off the street, demanding to see thirty or forty gems, asking for a lecture explaining once again what the four C's are, looking at every possible setting, finally picking one gem to be put in one ring, and then bringing it back a week later to be refit.

The jeweler has to charge more for the retail transaction for obvious reasons. So while you may get a lower price at "wholesale to the public" establishments, you're still purchasing at retail.

Q. *Now that you mention them, what are the four C's?*

A. Contrary to popular opinion, the Four C's are not a sixties doo-wop group but are instead the four traits of a diamond that give it its market value. In order, they are carat weight, color, clarity, and cut.

    Carat weight is the stone's actual weight. Put it on a scale and measure it. Do not confuse *carat,* the unit of gemstone weight, with *carat,* the measure of gold's purity, because they are unrelated. For the record, a gemstone carat (the unit of weight) equals 200 milligrams, or $\frac{1}{142}$ of an ounce. (For the record, in the case of carat as it relates to gold, the number of carats divided by 24 equals the proportion of gold in an alloy. Twelve-carat gold is 50 percent gold, 50 percent something else; 24-carat gold is just gold with no other impurities.

    Color refers to the color that the diamond appears to be when observed under a special white light. This is designated with a letter of the alphabet, *D* being best (and most expensive), *Z* being darkest.

    Cut is the only *C* put there by human beings and refers to the shaping that the diamond cutter gave the rough gem.

Brilliant-cut stones are the traditional shape, but there are many others, including pear-shaped, oval, and heart-shaped diamonds; the cut you choose is largely a matter of personal taste.

Clarity refers to how pure the crystal is. Diamonds are made of carbon (like coal and pencil lead) that has crystalized under extreme pressure. Some impurities remain in most stones. These are called by a variety of names, such as *clouds, feathers,* or *butterflies.* The Gemological Institute of America has instituted a standardized measure to rate clarity, ranging from FL (appears to be flawless under a jeweler's loupe) down to I3 (obviously marred). A better rating means fewer imperfections and a higher price.

Now, if you're going to buy a diamond engagement ring (and you do not have to) how do you choose? *Subjectively.* No matter what the diamond people say about appraisals and market value and so on, you are not going into the jewel business (most of you, anyway—if you are in the diamond business, you don't need this chapter). You are going to resell this gem only if things go tragically awry. You're purchasing a ring to wear, not as an investment. Be wary of buying "quality" that you cannot appreciate. The high end of the clarity scale and the high end of the color scale (FL and D, respectively) are largely for investors and diamond collectors and cost lots more money. Further, they can be distinguished from their less expensive brethren only by an expert. Your goal is to buy a nice ring that will be pretty to wear; if you don't lose sight of that goal, you'll hold your own in the deluge of gemological factoids.

Q. *Do I have to spend 2 months' pay on an engagement ring?*
A. No, but you should send 2 months' pay to the author of this book.

AMERICAN STOCK PHOTOGRAPHY

Q. *Does it have to be a diamond to be an engagement ring?*
A. No.

Q. *Can a man wear an engagement ring?*
A. Certainly. Though unusual, it's not unheard of and is the custom in some foreign countries, notably Germany. Most men wearing an engagement ring won't get the instant recognition from friends and strangers that women will, simply because few men wear engagement rings, so don't be disappointed when outsiders don't recognize its symbolism before you explain it to them.

Never forget that the entire drama and ordeal of purchasing a ring can be bypassed by using a family heirloom as an engagement ring.

Wedding Bands

Wedding bands are quite popular as a symbol of commitment and an outward sign of your marriage. The majority of couples today choose to wear them, and most of those incorporate the rings into the wedding ceremony itself. Wedding rings are often made of precious metal, usually an alloy of gold, silver, or platinum, or are family heirlooms. As with everything, many alternatives exist—like that chosen by Tommy Lee and Pamela Anderson Lee, who skipped rings altogether and had their respective ring fingers tattooed (and that didn't turn out so well).

Most couples select their wedding rings together, oftentimes choosing a matched set. If the bride (or both of you, as in Germany) wears an engagement ring, you probably want the wedding band to match.

Further, since many wedding bands look alike, consider having them engraved on the inside, perhaps with your initials and the date of the wedding, or with a secret and personal message. (For example, "*Baywatch* rules okay!" or "Motley Crüe Forever." Hmm. Maybe you'd be the best one to choose your own personal message.)

As with engagement rings, the value of a wedding band is in its function as a symbol of love and commitment and is fundamentally unrelated to the price. The richest man in America bought his wife's engagement ring at an Omaha department store (owned by the second-richest man in America).

Selecting a Jeweler

You want the same qualities in a jeweler that you want in a Boy Scout: trustworthiness, loyalty, friendliness, courtesy, kindness, obedience, bravery, thrift, cleanliness, and reverence. If you go through the yellow pages and call around, you're sure to find out that they all claim to be all those things.

Your task is to figure out who is telling the truth.

An engagement ring may be the single biggest expense before the wedding itself, and as such, the transaction will be fraught with tension. The best way to select a jeweler is to choose someone who comes recommended by a trusted friend or relative. If a sibling, teammate, or unindicted coconspirator whom you trust purchased a ring from a jeweler and had a good experience, you can benefit from his or her experience and go to the same place.

Remember always that you are the customer, and in these parts, anyway, the customer is always right. If you feel that the salesperson is pushy or not listening, you are in the wrong store. Stupid salesperson tricks that should send you running out of the store screaming include the following:

• A salesperson who refuses to explain things clearly. If you don't understand the difference between two jewels or between two rings and the dealer can't tell you the difference, it means either that the salesperson is obfuscating something that you might want to know or that the dealer really doesn't know. Either way, you lose.

• The "today only" special. A typical high-pressure tactic is to say that the big sale "ends today" or that the low, low prices will expire as soon as you leave the store. No matter how wise you are to these sorts of tricks, there's a residual suspicion that maybe, just this once, it's really true, and you blew a good deal by not jumping on it right then. Say it a hundred times: it's just a sales tactic.

• Dealers who want to sell you what they have in stock, instead of what you want. This old song goes something like this:

You: *We just got engaged, and we're interested in purchasing a diamond solitaire engagement ring.*

Dealer: *You're engaged? How cute! That's wonderful. I have some lovely ruby rings with diamond chips surrounding them that would be perfect.*

You: *No thanks. We really want the traditional ring.*

Dealer: *Are you sure you want to be so stuffy? The kids nowadays really like that ruby–diamond chip thing.*

You: *Yes. We know what we want.*

Dealer: *I could sell you a solitaire, but you'll regret it, believe you me.*

At this point you need say only one more word:

You: *Good-bye!*

• Indications that a company might not be there in a year. The surest sign that a company will continue in business 5 years down the road is if it was in business 5 years ago. Dealers who have been in business a long time have a relationship with the community and are more likely to give you a fair, honest deal. Now, of course, every jeweler started doing business at some time, and every one of them had to let someone be the first customer. That's true, of course; just let it be someone *else*.

• A salesperson who oversells. Wedding bands and engagement rings are purchased for the pleasure they bring. If a dealer starts stumping you with investment-speak ("I guarantee it will increase in value by forty-four percent in ten years") or attempts to harry you into a purchase you don't understand, stop. Take a deep breath. Remind yourself that purchasing a ring should be a pleasurable experience. If the dealer morphs into an evil car-dealer type of demon, walk out and find someone who knows what love is.

Chapter 4

Money

AMERICAN STOCK PHOTOGRAPHY

*T*here isn't enough money to go around.

You even had an argument or two about money and your wedding, maybe the worst one since you drew up the invitation list. Maybe it even ended in tears. Don't take it personally. If the wisenheimer writing *this* book long before your wedding knows you're having what the psychologists call "issues" about money, you can be sure everyone does. It's not a big deal, and it's not really about the amount of money you have to spend on your wedding, either. You may think, *If we had twice as much money, we'd be able to have the wedding we want.*

You'd be wrong. It's time to learn The Rule of Weddings and Money: *Weddings grow to consume all available funds. And keep on growing.*

If you have $1,000 budgeted for your wedding, your wedding will appear to require $2,000. If you have $1 million zillion in your budget, your wedding will appear to require $2 million zillion. People who got married "a while back" will only exacerbate the feeling that there isn't enough money as they tell you helpful things like "we had two mariachis and a hot-air balloon and fed four hundred people for only eight fifty plus tax." Yeah, uh-huh, sure. In 1934, maybe. They won't tell you they'd only budgeted $4.25.

This is not to advocate total surrender to the wedding vendors who are trying to suck money out of your individual and joint bank accounts; quite the opposite. Your ability to budget, to bargain with vendors, and to give up niceties you felt were "absolutely necessary" will be pushed to extremes while planning your wedding, and it'll *still* seem like you need more money. The important things are to remember that the wedding deficit is something that happens to everyone and to refrain from blaming each other—it's just one of those things.

The two of you should create a wedding budget as soon as possible. The first iteration of such a budget will be a jumping-off point; as new information flows your way, you can alter your figures, up until the point where you feel uncomfortable with the cost of the nuptials. Later in this chapter is a form that lists typical wedding expenses; you may use it to write in estimated figures or just as a list to jog your memory as to the kinds of expenditures that may be expected of you in the coming months.

If you prefer electronic budgeting, many computer programs are available to help you make an item-by-item budget for your wedding and then to track with remarkable precision exactly how far you have exceeded said budget. A hand-written paper budget offers the advantage of allowing you to maintain the illusion that you're within your budget for a much longer time.

Two schools of thought exist concerning how much to spend on your wedding: the "you only live once" school and the "it's only a wedding" school. The "you only live once" (also known as the "go for it") argument runs roughly as follows: "It's the specialest [*sic*] day ever and no expense should be spared. If we have a dime left in the bank or a buck on our credit line, we didn't do enough. Our wedding day is a turning point in our personal history, and it's not just for us; it's also for our family and friends. No matter how much money you have, everyone gets only one life to live. What is money for, if not to celebrate this holy occasion?"

The case for unrestrained expenditures is most compelling when someone else is footing the bills; but even those sensible, tightfisted Quicken addicts (and you know who you are) sometimes succumb to the siren call of "more is better for our wedding."

And that's okay.

And you're okay for thinking that way.

Examples of the "go for it" personality type are Elizabeth Taylor (eight weddings, each bigger than the last), Zorba the Greek, Bill Gates (guy rented an entire Hawaiian island), and Don Corleone (guy commissioned a couple of hits to celebrate his daughter's nuptials—and hits are not cheap).

The second group's motto might be "just because I fell in love doesn't mean I won the lottery" school of thought. These folks ask questions like "Will anyone really notice the difference between silk and nylon bows on the party favors?" and "Why should a video guy who works for half a day cost more than a video camera?" These types of deep philosophical questions challenge the heart of wedding budgeting. There are no right or wrong answers, and your particular responses will tell as much about your personal style as your blood type or the kind of car you drive.

The save-money argument runs like this: the money we spend on our wedding won't make us love each other any more than we already do. It won't improve us spiritually, it won't get us better friends or families, and it won't do much more than enrich the people who sell bridal doodads.

And that's okay.

And you're okay for thinking that way.

But . . . knew that was coming, didn't you?

Both arguments, carried to extremes, may produce a host of regrets. The "spend it—you only live once" crowd's regrets will come via the mail, a little more pain with each new bill. As though waking from a dream, they will examine the invoices in disbelief, as though *someone else* shelled out $14 a guest for hand-embroidered place holders, or $220 and change for velvet ropes to guide guests through the reception line. Some expenses, in hindsight, are bound to look silly, especially when you have to pay the hoodlums at the credit-card companies interest that runs as high as 21 percent per year.

Tightwads and Quicken geeks, you're getting very excited hearing about these excesses. You may be thinking of waving this chapter in your spouse-to-be's face and saying in a deep, clear voice, "See, I told you we can't spend so much. This book says so."

But financial regret isn't the only kind you might suffer. Those who shepherd every penny and purchase only "sensible" and "inexpensive" things may go through the opposite of buyer's remorse: call it "cheapskate's remorse," if you will. "Sensible" isn't the most appropriate sentiment when you get married; there really is nothing "sensible" about falling in love and/or getting married. It's the great mystery, the thing that keeps you going in spite of all the other nonsense in this crazy mixed-up world, and it's okay to cut loose a little.

The regret suffered by cutting too many corners can include friends and family whom you wish you'd invited but did not; music you wished you'd danced to but did not; flowers you wished were there but were not; or even the added fabulousness of a great hairstyle (or haircut).

The great balancing act is deciding how much is enough and how much is too much, and which is best accomplished by loud, heated arguments and name calling. After you reach an agreement, be sure to kiss and make up; it's only money.

A Wedding Budget

Preparing a budget for your wedding is actually fairly simple and provides an opportunity to discuss the scale and scope of the wedding you hope to have. The further in advance of the Big Day you discuss budgetary concerns, the easier it will be to remain level-headed and have only civilized arguments.

There are two types of wedding expenses: one-time and per-guest. Your **one-time** expenses include the rings, the license, the church, and so on. When the total of one-time expenses comes out too high, the only way to reduce it is to choose cheaper substitutes or do without one or more of the items. The **per-guest** expenses include meals, drinks, and so forth. You simply add up the amount of money that one guest would cost (dinner, snacks, drinks, etc.) and multiply it by the number of guests, and when you realize that that figure is unaffordable, you may either reduce the amenities provided each guest or go to chapter 6 ("The Invitation List") and reduce the number of guests.

Traditionally (which only means "in those other wedding books"), certain expenses are paid by the groom, certain expenses are paid by the bride, and other expenses are carried by the parents of the bride or groom. Remember also that you probably will find many items listed below that you don't need to purchase; when you come across such an item, it feels great to write a zero in that column.

A Wedding Budget May Include:

$_____ Bride's engagement ring

$_____ Groom's engagement ring

$_____ Engraving for engagement ring

$_____ Wedding bands

$_____ Engraving for wedding bands

$_____ A bridal consultant

$_____ Engagement party

$_____ Bridesmaids' luncheon

$_____ Rehearsal dinner

$_____ Reception

$_____ Printed invitations

$_____ Printed thank-you notes

$_____ Printed announcements

$_____ Stamps

$_____ Bridal gown

$_____ Bridal going-away clothes

$_____ Groom's formal wear

$_____ Groom's going-away clothes

$_____ Flowers for bride

$_____ Flowers for members of the wedding party

$_____ Catering for reception

$_____ Champagne

$_____ Wedding cake

$_____ Live music for ceremony

$_____ Live or recorded music for reception

$_____ Photographer

$_____ Videographer

$_____ 2 months' pay for author of this book

$_____ Marriage license

$_____ Fee for officiant

$_____ Honeymoon

$_____ Gifts for bridesmaids

$_____ Gifts for groomsmen

$_____ Hairstyling

$_____ Makeup

$_____ Rented automobiles/transportation

$_____ Guest book

After you arrive at a working total for your budget, add 15 percent under the category "things we never thought of." If you have to spend that additional money—and it's highly likely—then at least you have budgeted for it in advance. If you planned very carefully and never have to touch the 15 percent emergency reserve, then you'll have a windfall at the end of the wedding.

Where's All This Money Coming From, Anyway?

If one or both of you is personally paying for most or all of the wedding expenses, it becomes easier than ever to be ruthless about budget cutting. Suddenly, the $8-a-bottle champagne looks just as good as the $80-a-bottle champagne. And do we really need a lion tamer and Yo-Yo Ma at the reception? Maybe that money's better spent on something else.

However, if you are like the majority of couples getting married, someone else is going to help pitch in some cash to help out. Most likely it will be parents, but it might be grandparents, aunts and uncles, or even just a charitable friend. If this is your plan, be sure to bring it up as early as possible and have preliminary discussions about the scope and scale of commitment you can expect. Many ugly surprises will be avoided down the road if you explicitly discuss numbers early on.

If it's your parents who are coming to the rescue, remember that they're older than you are, and back in the old days when they got married, everything cost a fraction of what it costs now (or at least that's how they'll portray it to you). Be prepared for shock or even a coronary when you relay how much things actually cost in the real world. The conversation might go like this:

You: *We really appreciate your help, Mom and Dad.*
Your parents: *We're happy to pitch in. We'll pay for the photographer and the catering at the reception. Is that okay?*

Now, you could just nod your head yes and let it go at that, until they get the bill. But in the spirit of free and open disclosure, it might be better to put a number on that unspecified commitment. The conversation after that might sound something like this:

You: *That would be terrific. Thank you so much. We've already talked to the photographer and several caterers, and we have a rough idea how much they'd cost.*

Your parents: *At our wedding, we paid fifty dollars for a top photographer and six dollars a head for catering.*

This is the point where illusion will collide with reality; it's time to apprise them of the way the world has changed:

You: *Yes, but you got married in 1967.*

Your parents (reminiscing): *Ah, yes, the summer of love. Your mother and I were married at Woodstock, wearing nothing but mud and beads and flowers—*

You (retching at the thought): *We think we'll go for a church. And things cost more nowadays—*

Your parents: *How much more?*

You: *Photographer's going to charge six hundred fifty dollars. And catering's twenty a head.*

This is where your parents act shocked. Play along. Feel their pain. Ask them how much a new car cost when they got married and how much one costs nowadays. That'll get 'em really nostalgic. And then close the deal:

Your parents: *Okay.*

You: *We're counting on you.*

Your parents: *Wanna hear my Big Brother and the Holding Company albums?*

You're on your own with that one.

If you've put together a budget, gone to every possible source of funding, and found that the expense column is overwhelming the income column, be prepared to do some cutting. Cuts can come in two forms: either get a similar item for less or skip the expense altogether. It's never pleasant to omit something that you'd hoped to include, but better to be honest about it up front than to be saddled with bills you can't handle just as you're starting your marriage.

Also remember that even if it's not the root of all evil, money is the source of many marital conflicts. Get used to discussing it now. For many people, a discussion of money just makes their stomach tighten up; it's stressful and unpleasant and who wouldn't rather talk about sports or astrology instead? (In fact, some people would rather sing "The Star-Spangled Banner" naked in front of a televised audience than discuss money. Those people have bigger problems than we can deal with in this book.)

But talk about the budget. Get it over with. Marital intimacy isn't only about the sex (as important as that is); it's about sharing the kinds of secret concerns that we can't share with anyone else, and that may include money. Turn any cuts in your wedding wish list into a bonding experience and come out feeling closer and happier than ever: "I love you more than ever, honeybunny, but we just can't afford the jugglers."

Chapter 5

Gifts

One of the big material differences between getting married and "just living together" is the sheer volume of cash and prizes that are rained down on marrying couples, almost as if they've won a game show. The goodwill of your friends and loved ones truly goes above and beyond the call of duty around the time of your nuptials. You'll have certain obligations to ensure (1) that gift givers are giving you something that you genuinely wish to receive and (2) that you appreciate their generosity. Before discussing the strategy and logistics of gift giving it may be worthwhile to examine the perplexing enigma you both may be wondering about.

Why Are All These Nice People Giving Us All This Great Stuff?

Your wedding is a rite of passage, one of the most important toll booths on life's interstate. And it may just be the happiest of all rites of passage: consider that others include birth (too messy and painful to be much fun), your first day of school (too fleeting to be memorable), and death (hardly a cause for celebration). To those who know and love you, your wedding day represents the fulfillment of their hopes for you. The two of you found each other, fell in love, and avoided all the sorts of unpleasantness that might have derailed you before this happy event.

Your wedding will therefore resonate with others in your community for a variety of reasons: some, because it reminds them of the deep satisfaction that their own wedding inaugurated; others, because they'll never marry for one reason or another and the unique love a married couple shares is something they may enjoy only vicariously. The hopes and dreams of your community are projected on you on your wedding day, and the giver of a gift can share in some small way the magic that exists between the two of you.

Thus, wedding gifts are almost as much for the giver as they are for the recipient; the personal association that a gift carries is as important as its day-to-day practicality. Durable housewares—dishes, linens, silverware, and so on—are traditional wedding gifts for a very good reason. Each time you pull out "the soup tureen Aunt Ellen gave us" or "the kitchen knives Fred gave us," you are reminded of the goodwill and love expressed by the person who gave you the gift. In a palpable way, the connection between your marriage and your community is reaffirmed.

And that's pretty important.

Back to Reality

All this heavy symbolism is moot unless you learn the right way to get all this deeply meaningful *stuff* from them and to the two of you. These practical matters matter.

The Registry

What if you could walk through a department store (or look through a catalog) and pick all the *stuff* you want in your dream home? Well, guess what? You can. What a pleasant surprise.

Department stores, catalog companies, and even some sporting goods and specialty stores offer bridal registry services to act as a liaison between the marrying couple and their

$\mathcal{I}$ think it's a miniature Stanley Cup. Do you have relatives in Canada?"

AMERICAN STOCK PHOTOGRAPHY

well-wishers. A gift registry is initiated when the two of you visit the store and schlep from department to department, indicating which items you would enjoy receiving. Then, as people who are invited to your wedding visit the store, clerks will guide them to purchase gifts from your list. If someone has already chosen an identical item, the clerk will encourage them to choose another.

What's in it for the store? Thousands of dollars in sales for the measly cost of keeping up a list. Weddings and wedding registries are a multibillion-dollar business and department stores compete fiercely with each other so that you'll select them as your registry. If you've already filed for your wedding license or filled out a reader reply card from a bridal magazine, chances are some stores may have contacted you already. "Free bridal fair" is a typical lure. The department store will offer a seminar that includes "informative product lectures" followed by a free box lunch, a fashion show, and usually door prizes. These bridal shows can actually be lots of fun. (Well, maybe the fashion show's fun. The product lectures are often a lot like infomercials, except you can't change the channel because there's some poor schmo standing there trying to convince you why you need to spend $700 on a cappuccino machine.) Usually the only price of admittance to one of these shows is—you guessed it—that you register with that particular store.

Although indeed it costs *you* nothing to register (and you get a free lunch!), you shouldn't select the store you register with on the basis of the lavishness of their bridal fair. Remember always that relatives and loved ones will pay for your gifts (and indirectly for your "free" lunch.) If the store is a rip-off joint, your wedding guests will be ripped off. When selecting a store with which to register, put yourself in your invitees' shoes. Is it easy to do business with said establishment? Are their prices fair? Is the service good? Nothing is more frustrating than entering a huge department store intending to drop a bunch of money on a wedding gift and blowing an hour trying to locate a salesperson.

Alternative Registries

Some couples feel that household goods aren't to their liking and yet still want to receive wedding gifts. These couples create alternative registries: perhaps in support of some hobby (e.g., mountain climbing, competitive dentistry, or guns and ammo) or even have the audacity to suggest that wedding guests express their generosity by putting cash in an account designated for a major purchase, such as a house, car, or even the honeymoon. Carefully consider the meaning of wedding gift giving before pursuing such an alterno-registry. Asking for cash sounds a little greedy no matter how good the cause. Someone who gives you a toaster oven knows that you'll be thinking of him or her every time you eat toast; someone who gives you cash can't point to the front window of your home and say, "The one hundred fifty dollars I gave them paid for seventy-one percent of these window blinds."

Registering for oddball items may be appropriate if all of your guests share a similar enthusiasm, but it still may lack the sentimental kick of housewares—the gifts that keep on reminding you of the giver. If you already have all the housewares you need—for example, if this will be the second marriage for one or both of you—perhaps the most tasteful way to allow well-wishers to express their generosity is to set up a charity donation account for a good cause in your community.

Catalogs

Many catalogs now offer a registry service. They often carry the same or similar inventory as the large department stores and often at a deep discount. Such catalog companies usually advertise in the popular bridal magazines. A mail-order registry can be especially handy if your friends and relatives are scattered over a wide geographical area. Make sure it offers a "100 percent satisfaction guarantee" and a liberal returns policy in case you receive duplicates or defective items.

Getting the Word Out

Okay. You've gone to some bridal fairs and checked out a few catalogs, decided what kinds of gifts you would like to receive, and registered with a company that has fair prices and good service. Now you just get on the telephone and tell everyone you have invited to the wedding, "We registered with the such-and-such company; go buy us a gift." Right?

Wrong.

Though etiquette obliges anyone invited to your wedding to give you a wedding gift, etiquette also obliges you to behave as if you're not *expecting* that gift. Each new package should be a pleasant surprise, a measure of the unforced generosity of the giver.

The natural question remains How the heck do they find out where you registered? Well, though you cannot preemptively announce where you've registered, it's okay to tell someone if he or she asks directly. Similarly, though it is verboten for *you* to shout it from the mountaintop and put it on your web site, your parents, family, and friends can diplomatically and quietly spread the word. Etiquette and protocol are very strange.

The Gifts Themselves

Now begins the part of the book where we reveal some of the closely held secrets that are revealed only to married (and soon-to-be-married) couples. By reading the following, you agree to keep it tippy-top secret, allowing single people to marvel at the knowledge that you have accumulated but never sharing it with them. After all, as a soon-to-be-married couple, you have to keep your edge over the single horde.

Fine silver is 99.9 percent pure silver, abbreviated chemically with the symbol *Ag*. Unfortunately, pure silver is too soft to make good dinnerware.

Sterling silver is an alloy of 92.5 percent silver and 7.5 percent copper. The copper provides the hardness necessary to make good silverware.

Electroplating is a process by which a thin coat of silver is deposited on a less expensive metal. The metal underneath is usually an alloy of nickel, copper, and zinc.

Glass is made from silica (sand) and potash or soda. It was invented by the Egyptians in the fifteenth century B.C.

Crystal is glass to which lead oxide is added, in addition to sand and potash. It is also known as **leaded glass. Half-lead** contains 24 percent lead oxide, and **full-lead** contains 30 percent oxide. (Don't ask how 24 equals half of 30; that's for the advanced class.)

Pressed glass may look like cut glass but is usually less expensive. Running your finger over pressed glass will usually reveal a seam where the mold halves were joined.

Cut glass, on the other hand, is seamless. (Don't search for a seam in front of your guests. In fact, it's tactless to do it at all, but people do anyway.)

Bone china really does contain bones. The ash of calcined bones is mixed in with the porcelain, making a harder, more valuable dish.

Pewter is 91 percent tin, 7 percent antimony, and 2 percent copper. Antique pewter may contain lead, but modern pewter does not.

Brass is made of copper and zinc.

Who Gets to Decide What to Register For

The human capacity for bickering knows no limits.

Imagine this: two people, in love with one another, decide to get married. Then, all their friends and relatives decide to give them nice gifts. Is this grounds for an argument?

Unfortunately, yes, it is. You may be the luckiest people in the world and yet still find time to engage in trench warfare about whether to have the trendy-looking dinner pattern or the old-fashioned kind that's been in the family for years. It seems that if life is going to have *some* problems, the kinds of problems you want are choosing between dinnerware patterns. Can this argument be avoided?

Maybe. Maybe not.

The gifts you've registered for are a way of asserting your taste, style, and values. On the surface each choice may appear insignificant: who cares if we have the shiny silver toaster instead of the white porcelain version decorated with ducks?

But after about 40 such decisions, the wife-to-be and the husband-to-be may discover gaps in their taste and style. Such gaps can generate a little premarital tension as each party silently wonders what the heck they're doing:

She: *Do I really want to marry a man who thinks a good stereo is more important than an elegant couch?*

He: *Do I really want to marry a woman who could pass up an opportunity to assemble the best stereo ever built?*

And so on.

When registering, keep an open dialogue. You're never going to have the same tastes, a lesson that is reinforced repeatedly during the gift-registration process. Remember: anything is subject to negotiation. If agreement is impossible on some subject, perhaps swap entire categories; for example, you pick out all the linens and I'll pick out all the tableware. That way, both of you had a say in some part of the house. The worst is if you begin wanting different things and wind up with something neither of you wants:

Him: *Let's register for a set of martini glasses.*
Her: *Martini glasses? We never drink martinis. Why not register for something we might actually use, like egg poachers?*
Him: *I'll go for the egg poachers if you go for the martini glasses.*
Her: *I don't like poached eggs.*
Him: *Why did you want egg poachers?*
Her: *I don't. I just don't want martini glasses either.*

And so on; you can see how pretty soon they'll be registering for a whole set of stuff that belongs in someone else's life. If one of you really, truly wants something that the other does not, stick to your guns—unless you want to risk winding up owning dozens of egg poachers that no one wants.

Thank-You Notes

Every gift must be acknowledged with a handwritten thank-you note. Let's say it again—all together, please: *Every gift must be acknowledged with a handwritten thank-you note.* Seems simple enough, but let's examine the sentence phrase by phrase to make sure the point is hammered home.

Every gift must be acknowledged . . . means just that— not some, not most. If one relative sends two separate gifts, and you've already written a note for the first when the second arrives—write a second note. If four members of a family send four different gifts, you have to write four different notes. Get it? No exceptions.

. . . with a hand-written . . . Some computer-savvy peo-

$\mathcal{D}$ear Uncle Bob,

Thank you for the lovely particle accelerator. We'll think of you each time we discover a new subatomic particle . . ."

AMERICAN STOCK PHOTOGRAPHY

ple believe that it's equally polite to send e-mail, or a hand-some laser-printed reply. They are wrong. You could have the best-looking laser printer in the world, hooked up to the fastest microprocessor in the world, running the world's best software, and if you used it to write a thank-you note, you'd still be wrong, whereas a chump with a fifty-cent ballpoint pen and a sheet of white paper, writing a similar thank-you note, would be right. The point conveyed when the generous person who gave the gift receives your note is that you sat down, pen in hand, and wrote them a nice note.

. . . **thank-you note.** What goes in a thank-you note? The usual system for writing thank-you notes is to first purchase a special pen, especially for writing thank-you notes. Then, purchase special paper—cute little cards—that are especially for writing thank-you notes. Next, clean out the refrigerator. After that, perhaps a telephone call to some close friends. When it's good and late, stare at the huge stack of blank thank-you cards a while. Maybe have a glass of milk—low-fat; don't want to gain weight before the wedding—and then get out that special pen and you may learn a weird lesson: It's hard to think of something to say.

Don't worry about it. The note itself is as important as its content. Simple can be better. The classic thank-you note runs roughly as follows:

Dear Aunt Sarah,

Thank you for the garden tools. Kelly and I are planning to grow tomatoes this summer (after the wedding, of course) and the hoe will be especially handy for working the soil. Perhaps we'll bring some tomatoes by your house; needless to say, we'll be thinking of you when we are out gardening. We look forward to seeing you at the wedding!

Love,

Pat

A few simple lines, sign it, stick it in the envelope, and you're done. If you invited a lot of people to your wedding, you can expect a lot of gifts. Don't let the thank-you notes build up to the point where you're feeling overwhelmed. And most of all: keep a log of who gave you what. Nothing is as embarrassing as thanking the wrong party for a gift given to you by someone else.

Chapter 6

The
Invitation List

*E*ach of you has a best friend whom you believe absolutely must be invited to the wedding. But then there's that second-best friend, who must be invited as well—no use alienating that friend by letting on that he or she occupies the number-two position. But then you've got that friend who's almost as close as number two . . . why not invite that friend, too? Avoid the big hassle.

You keep going down that road and at some point you run into trouble. If it's a big wedding, you might have a line somewhere between your fifty-fifth closest friend, who gets the invitation, and your fifty-sixth closest friend, who didn't make the cut.

Then there's the matter of relatives. Invite your parents? Unless there's bad blood between you, of course you want to invite your parents. Siblings? Yes, certainly. Aunts and uncles? Sure, invite them on down. Grandparents? It'll be the happiest day of their lives. But pretty soon you get into the weird shirt-tail relatives. The son of the woman whom your uncle married and then divorced, who doesn't come around much anymore and always smelled like wood chips? The second cousin who speaks with a Lithuanian accent even though he was born and raised in Kentucky? Eventually you'll encounter a relative whose relation itself is a source of some mystery:

Him: *Freddy? Isn't he in Dawn and Chuck's family?*
Her: *No, not that I know of.*
Him: *Well, then he must be one of Pietra's ex-husbands.*

Her: *Don't think so. She was married to Andy, then Petruccio, then Jerome . . . never was a Freddy in that list.*
Him: *Is he related?*
Her: *He always comes to Thanksgiving.*
Him: *Do we have to invite him to the wedding?*
Her: *If we can't figure out how he's related, why would we invite him to the wedding?*
Him: *Maybe someone we know better will be miffed if we don't invite him.*
Her: *Okay, what's his last name?*
Him: *Uhh . . .*

Here's a rule of thumb: if you don't know how you're related, you don't have to invite that person. Unless you want to.

But even if you're on good terms with everyone you've ever met, there will be some limits to the number of people who may attend your wedding. Taste, space, and money all play a part in cutting down the number of people you can invite. Taste because at some point, the two of you will sit down and decide exactly how big a wedding you want to have and what kind of venue you want to have it in; and unless that venue is the Astrodome, there will likely be more people you want to invite to the wedding than available space.

The realization that there's only a finite number of people that can be invited to your wedding is inevitably a difficult one. Find out that number early. Whether you determine that you'll have 15 guests or 5,000, the earlier you know what that number is, the better. Why? Because then you can begin doing what people in politics call "managing perceptions." Especially if your guest list will be smaller than you had hoped—which happens more often than not—you can put out the word that you won't be able to invite everyone in the

If you can't determine precisely how that distant relative is related, you're not obliged to invite him to the wedding.

AMERICAN STOCK PHOTOGRAPHY

physical universe. "Managing perceptions" is a recent concept that is illustrated by an old joke that goes as follows:

> *A couple leaving on vacation ask a neighbor to take care of their cat. The neighbor agrees. After their vacation is half over, the vacationers call the neighbor to ask how the cat is doing. The neighbor tells them, "Your cat died."*
>
> *"How?"*
>
> *"Just died. I don't know."*
>
> *The bluntness of the response, more than anything else, bothered the caller. "You shouldn't have told us just like that. We need to be warmed up for bad news like that," said the cat owner.*
>
> *"What did you want me to say?"*
>
> *"Well, when we called, you could have said something like 'Your cat's on the roof and he won't come down.' Then, when we called in a couple of days, you could have said, 'I called the fire department and they can't get the cat off the roof.' Then we'd be ready for the bad news when we called later and you told us the cat was dead."*
>
> *"Well, sorry. I should have warmed you up."*
>
> *"It's okay," said the vacationer. "The cat was old, anyway. Has anything else happened while we were away?"*
>
> *"Well, nothing much else happened, except your mother's on the roof and she won't come down."*

It's a corny joke, but it illustrates an important principle: never let your neighbor take care of your cat. Actually, that's not so important; the important principal is that you should warm people up for the possibility of bad news. Without being so blunt, it helps if, in early conversations about your wedding, you let potential guests know that some people whom you love dearly won't be invited. You'll get a double benefit: first, those who get invited will feel especially lucky. "I made the cut," they'll believe. And those who didn't get invited won't feel so bad. They will have prepared themselves in advance for the possibility that their cat is on the roof and it won't come down—or that they may not get invited, as much as you'd like to invite them.

Let's review. You've figured out approximately how many people you can invite to the wedding. Then, you *managed perceptions* by letting everyone know that there will be a few people who don't get invited to the wedding. All that's left is a knock-down drag-out fight about who makes the cut and who doesn't.

Why a fight, and why now? You may pick one of the following reasons:

1. Because in the general excitement of the wedding, both of you may invite more people than can be accommodated, and the embarrassment of doing so can lead to hurt feelings and even an argument.
2. Because we live in an era of diminished expectations, and the scarcity of resources—in this case, invitations to the wedding—have stressed the interpersonal relationship between the two of you.
3. Because one of you would rather call the whole thing off than invite that no-good lazy bum—let's not even name names here because everyone knows whom we're talking about—that your spouse-to-be wants to invite.

If you answered any of the above, you get a prize of your own choosing. (The prize is in the fridge—help yourself.)

The truth is, sorting out the invitation list is never easy. Let's say the two of you visited wedding sites, found one you loved, did the math, and determined that you could invite a total of 100 people to the wedding. Sounds like a lot, doesn't it?

Well, you may go through a thought process something like this: *if we have a hundred invitations, I'll get half—that's fifty*

$\mathscr{D}$ouble-check to ensure that the site you have chosen for the reception can accommodate all the guests that you've invited.

AMERICAN STOCK PHOTOGRAPHY

people. Then you start counting how many friends, relatives, and so on that you have, and it gets to 50 pretty quickly. (If it were 200, it'd get there pretty quickly, too.) Then, suddenly, you remember that about a third of the people you want to invite have husbands or wives who need inviting as well (yes, you *must* invite the spouse). So your 50 becomes 60 or 70; and your future spouse has gone through the same thought processes and come up with 60 or 70 people as well. So you add them together and are shocked to learn that you're up to 130 people.

Then, you talk to your parents. And your spouse's parents. And discover that there are another 40 or 50 "must invite" people, and some of them have spouses, and now for your 100-person venue you've got to invite about two hundred people.

Oops.

What to do now?

Start making apologies, explanations, and justifications.

Or better yet, plan ahead. Make a preliminary list early in discussions. Talk about it. Put all the names on the same page. Ask for input from others . . . all before sending out a single invitation. So with the theoretical 100-person limit, you can be safe starting out with 60 or 70 names; when you add wives and husbands and people you have to invite (but don't necessarily think of in the first session of drawing up names), you will find that you're pretty close to the original estimate.

Interpersonal Conflicts

There is a certain group of people whom neither one of you wants to invite but wind up with an invitation nonetheless. The way they wind up at your wedding is as mysterious as how Jell-O is made, but there are some theories. The three leading explanations are as follows:

1. *Those people invited themselves.* This happens far more often than anyone likes to acknowledge. Usually it comes in the form of a chance meeting. For example, one of you is at the library and happens to run into one of those people whom you recognize but can't remember why. While you're racking your brains trying to figure out who it is (*Is it my lab partner from high school? Someone I know from work? Maybe someone that I used to see at church?*), you nervously make small talk. Without thinking, you blather out the most exciting thing to happen lately—"I'm getting married!" and the person you're talking with suddenly behaves as if a casual reference to your wedding is the same as an invitation to said wedding. Because you are too polite, you refrain from pointing out "I don't even know who the heck you are, much less want to invite you to my wedding," by which time the person has already pried details of when and where from you. Be prepared for such an ambush. If you wind up with one such oddball at your wedding, *c'est la vie* (a French phrase that, translated, literally means "what a doofus I am to let that person wrangle an invitation from my hand"). If it happens twice, you're in real trouble.

How should you handle such a situation? The world is filled with people who don't have any sympathy for your troubles trying to pare down the guest list at your wedding, who try to invite themselves or act hurt when they find out that maybe they won't go. What do you say to them? "We're not inviting you, pal" is a little too harsh and makes you sound too much like Don Johnson on *Miami Vice*. Perhaps it's more appropriate to say "We're having a hard time inviting as many people as we'd like to; we're sorting out the invitation list now. If you don't get an invitation, it's not because we didn't want you there." Then, later, you can discover what you already knew, which is that there just wasn't room.

$\int$ometimes, people just mysteriously show up at the wedding and there's nothing you can do about it.

AMERICAN STOCK PHOTOGRAPHY

2. *Those mystery wedding guests didn't invite themselves, but they weren't invited by anyone else, either; they assumed that it's okay just to show up at a wedding the same way you might show up at a house party.* "The more the merrier!" they believe, and although that may be true in certain circumstances, the strategic planning that goes into a wedding makes it difficult for just anyone to show up. If you catch wind in advance that there will be unwitting wedding crashers, it may be wise to put out the word, through a trusted third party, that they really weren't invited. If a few of these folks just turn up on the day of the wedding, it's too late to do anything; just smile and remember it's your big day.

3. *There are some people you are scared* not *to invite.* Anyone who has seen the animated movie *Sleeping Beauty* knows that had the bad witch been invited to the party, she wouldn't have put the curse on Sleeping Beauty.* This story haunts some people, and when planning their wedding, they invite a person or two simply because they're scared of the ramifications were they not to invite them. Resist the temptation. First of all, why have someone you don't want at your wedding, at your wedding? Second—witches don't exist. Give the bad guys the day off. Make it your day. Which leads us to . . .

People Not to Invite

Don't invite people with whom you hope to settle a score. The classic example is an ex-boyfriend or ex-girlfriend. *See—you dumped me, but look what happened since then! I'm getting married! Ah-hahahahaha.*

Don't invite troublemakers. You know who they are—

---

*This account is according to the bad witch herself, who, being bad, shouldn't be trusted. But that's another story.

Garth Brooks called them "friends in low places"—and even after you're married, you can still count on them for hooting and hollering, but maybe it's better to give them the weekend off when it's time to get married.

Use great caution when inviting both halves of a divorced couple. Sometimes you want to have both the ex-husband and the ex-wife at a wedding, but remember that tensions run high between such people. If you go through with the decision to invite such a (former) couple, alert your ushers to their presence and have them seated far, far away from each other.

My Half, Your Half, and Everyone Else's Half

The negotiations to determine who gets invited to your wedding and who doesn't may be slightly more involved than the strategic nuclear arms treaties. Here's a forum in which your differences of opinion go from being abstractions to being friends with names and faces. Each of you will undoubtedly have strong opinions about who can be invited and who cannot. Make up individual lists, get suggestions from your parents, if they're playing a role in planning the wedding, and then lock yourselves in for a long night of negotiations.

Disconnect the phone.

Get some pizza and soda.

Pull out your lists.

And begin. Get over the shock that you've invited too many people. Then each of you has to get over the shock that your spouse-to-be invited someone you would just as soon never see again. (It happens.) Then pick a target number and begin paring down the list. Begin by pulling out all the names of people who absolutely, positively must be invited. Put the letter *A* next to those names. Count them up. With luck, you won't have exceeded your quota of wedding guests yet; if you have, then you have a lot of work ahead of you. If you still have spots left, subtract the number of people who have to be invited from the total number of guests you can accommodate. This number is the *available slots;* compare it with the names who didn't rate an *A,* then start cutting. In an ideal world, you'd invite them all; but then again, in an ideal world, you'd have a few mansions, a private business jet, your own island in the Caribbean, and a staff to maintain it all. You don't, so you have to pare down your guest list, never a fun job. Maybe some rules of thumb will help determine who makes the cut and who doesn't. When you come to a friend who might not be invited, ask yourself these questions:

1. Have you ever been invited to that person's house or apartment? If not, maybe it's not so big a disappointment for him or her not to be invited to your wedding.
2. Is the prospective invitee a friend you have known for a long time? Oftentimes, the people in the gray area are just buddies from work; if you think that these friendships would be over if one of you changed jobs, then it's not so bad to omit these friends from the wedding list (if you have to).

These rules of thumb may help you eliminate some names; if you're like most people, a surplus will still exist. These are the hardest people to cut; no one wants to, but it's a part of being a grown-up. Just hang together, grit your teeth, and pare down that list. If you are decisive early on, your life will be much easier down the road.

Padding the Guest List

Even after a long night of cutting, it's not at all unusual to end up with a surplus of people who cannot be accommodated.

Don't panic (yet); there is a way to pad your guest list without anyone noticing. Your absolute limit is on the number of people who can *attend* your wedding; but the crisis comes when you're trying to slim down the number of people you can *invite*. In this little distinction lies a loophole you may begin taking advantage of immediately.

Here's the math. Some of the people you invite will not be able to attend. Maybe they're out of town; maybe they're sick; maybe they're due to give birth around the time of your wedding. Any way you slice it, there will be a few people who politely decline your invitation.

Sometimes, you can guess who that will be in advance. A beloved relative who is confined to a distant hospital will obviously not be able to attend; you can send such an invitation with impunity. But such clear-cut no's are few and far between; far more common are the people who may or may not come. Maybe they live far away but have always wanted to come to the city where the wedding will take place. What're the odds those people will attend? Fifty–fifty? Maybe there's another potential guest who has to go to Bora Bora on business but might be able to delay the trip? You could give that one a 60–40? A 1 in 10? A snowball's chance in—

Well, you get the point. There are potential guests who have some probability of coming. This is where you can pad your guest list. Separate all the names of people who might (or might not) come and assign each a percentage:

Aunt Alice and Uncle Pete—50% chance that they'll come
Uncle Bill—25%
Chuck from school—75%
Dana from work—90%
Ukbar from Urantia—10%

So, from the list above you could reasonably guess that of the six invitations you send out, three will attend. This gambit, carefully employed, allows you to honor friends and family with an invitation without the fear that everyone invited will attend and overflow the church (or bowling alley or whichever lovely spot you've chosen). You may discover that you can *invite* a 120 people and reasonably guess that only 90 will *attend.*

Dates

There are a few groups of people who automatically are expected to bring a date to your wedding. These are as follows:

- *Disabled guests.* If a guest is disabled and requires an assistant (for example, to push a wheelchair), then that assistant should also be invited.
- *Those who are married.* If you invite one half of a married couple, the spouse is automatically invited; the invitation should include the name of the spouse. If in your haste you neglected to put both names on the invitation, mail the forgotten spouse an invitation as soon as the error is noticed.
- *Engaged couples.* Engaged couples get two separate invitations, but if you're inviting one half, you should invite the other.

That's the end of the list. Unless your invitation specifies so, the rest of the people you invite are not expected to bring dates. A few will bring dates anyway, of course—but they're not supposed to. Again, if someone shows up with a new hot (uninvited) date on his or her arm at your wedding, it's too late to do anything about it.

Wording Choices and Buying Invitations

The wording of invitations is a fairly straightforward proposition, and most of the companies who print invitations will help you in that regard. Some of the "traditional" invitation wording choices may sound a little stuffy, but since your union is scheduled to last "until death do us part," traditional may be a better choice than, say, quoting Beck lyrics. A suitable list of printers can be found either in the yellow pages of the town where you live or in the advertisements featured in the stack of bridal magazines over there in the corner.

Preprinted invitations are expensive; engraved preprinted invitations, even more so. If your budget is stretching at the seams, remember that the "most proper" type of invitation is handwritten—not preprinted at all.

If both of you have bad handwriting, you may want to engage the services of a calligrapher when addressing envelopes. If that is too expensive, maybe just ask for help from a friend with beautiful handwriting. And remember: it always takes twice as long to address envelopes as you think it will.

Chapter 7

Religion

*I*n love songs, on television, and in movies, couples always get married in a chapel or a church and no one ever asks exactly what kind of chapel or church it is.

In real life, people of different religious backgrounds often fall in love and get engaged; then it comes time to choose *where* to tie the knot, and suddenly, the religious differences that didn't seem like such a big deal loom large over the proceedings. Visions of childhood religious instruction suddenly come back to haunt each of you and the question of how to raise the children seems like it must be solved immediately.

Crisis? Or bump in the premarital road?

Spiritual Issues Matter

The good news is that almost every religion encourages and promotes marriage. The Catholic church and some others even consider marriage a sacrament, on a par with holy communion and baptism.

If you choose to have a religious ceremony, advance planning will help ensure that your wedding is everything you dreamed of. Especially if you want to marry in a church, synagogue, or temple, advance notice is critical. No matter how good your intentions, once a house of worship has been booked by someone else, you may be out of luck. The safest policy is to propose a range of possible dates with your officiant (that's what we call the rabbi, priest, or minister who will be officiating the ceremony), then select the date and plan the rest of the wedding festivities around that. All too often, couples set a date, notify family and friends, print and mail invitations, and then learn that their desired site is unavailable. But you two—you're smarter than that. That will never happen to you.

Every faith and every individual clergyperson has rules about what can and cannot be done in a particular house of worship. Some faiths refuse to perform marriages outside the house of worship itself; others have restrictions on which days of the week weddings may occur. In the first meeting with your officiant, ask enough questions that at the end of the meeting you can answer at least the following:

1. What premarital counseling is required?
2. What days are the officiant and the prospective wedding site available?
3. What costs will we be asked to pay? (Any "suggested donation" is a hard-and-fast cost—refusing to pay it is inconsiderate.) Is there an additional fee for church musicians to perform?
4. Can we choose our own music?
5. Can we change the words of the ceremony? (Some clerics are adamant about using the traditional ceremony; others don't mind the personal involvement of those getting married.)
6. Will there be a sermon? Can we suggest a topic?
7. If the two of you are of different religious faiths, can clergy from both beliefs officiate jointly?
8. Are there any rules about the religious beliefs of the attendants and/or guests who will be allowed to attend the wedding?

You may be surprised at how knowledgeable and comfortable with weddings your officiant is. Chances are, your minister, priest, or rabbi has performed many weddings in the past, has watched many marriages take root and thrive, and watched as others founder. Listen carefully; you may learn something about your wedding, or even more important, you may learn something about marriage. Which brings us to the next topic . . .

Premarital Counseling

You may have believed that marital counseling was only for couples who are in trouble, but you'd be surprised to discover that many churches now require counseling for couples *before* they marry, and before any troubles arise. For some couples, the prospect of counseling can be daunting. *What are they going to ask us? Are they going to taunt me for my spotty church attendance record? Will I have to take a test of religious knowledge? Is there any spanking involved?* Rabbis, priests, and ministers are scary in part because they're so often associated with times and places of crisis: they always show up at funerals, at hospitals, and during times of war and national disaster. But they have knowledge and experience to share; in fact, counseling may turn out to be the time best spent during your wedding preparation.

If your faith requires counseling, expect frank discussions about subjects that are most important to the success of your marriage. These are subjects that you'd expect a marrying couple had already discussed in depth, but that's not always the case, like whether or not to have children; life goals; where to live; where you see yourselves in 5 years, in 10 years, in 25 years. These aren't the kinds of topics that spontaneously come up in conversation. That's why the somewhat formal setting of counseling, with a third person there, helps get everything out in the open. For some questions, there are no right or wrong answers, but simply having a discussion about them helps.

Some faiths require that a couple attend a weekend seminar, such as Engaged Encounter, before the ceremony. Sacrificing two days of movies and football games just to get married may seem a high price, but those who have attended report mostly favorable comments about such sessions.

Engaged Encounter is a sister program to Marriage Encounter, which was developed in Spain and imported to America in the 1960s. The seminar was originally only for Catholics, but now variations are offered by other faiths. The focus is on helping couples develop strong communication skills, with the goal of making their marriage a stronger partnership.

Although the activities vary at the discretion of the individual group leaders, you can expect to go through exercises aimed at helping you learn more about each other. Topics that are always included are marriage morality, becoming a family, signs of a closed relationship, decisions in marriage, and sex and sexuality—all important life skills or topics that, once learned or discussed, can only make your marriage a stronger one.

What If We're of Different Religions?

In a nation with thousands of different denominations in dozens of different religions, it is inevitable that two human beings raised in different traditions will fall in love with each other. It happens all the time, and it has happened all the time for as long as there have been men and women. Romeo and Juliet fell in love, didn't they? (But don't emulate their example—both of 'em were dead inside a week.) What happens now? Will you both burn in hell? What happens if one of you is an agnostic and the other a dyslexic?*

Some religious groups will not perform interfaith mar-

---

*For one thing, you may have children who aren't sure if dogs exist.

riages at all, others allow them only if the outsider converts, and others see no conflict in marrying any two people who love each other regardless of their religious beliefs. If there will be a problem, you'll hear about it the first time you approach the clergyperson.

Merely ignoring the question and opting for a civil ceremony (maybe performed by an Elvis impersonator in Vegas) will only delay the inevitable. If either of you has deeply held religious convictions, better to discuss them before you tie the knot. Deciding how children should be raised is not a question to answer when they're in diapers.

You won't (necessarily) burn in hell, but your time here on earth may be a little hotter. Don't let religious differences split the two of you apart, though. Discuss the subject frankly and openly, and make any necessary accommodations and compromises in advance. There are many happily married couples who worship differently during the entire course of their marriages. Just don't ignore the subject, hoping it will go away. It won't.

Chapter 8

The Law

AMERICAN STOCK PHOTOGRAPHY

*T*he law? What's the law got to do with getting married? "A wedding is supposed to be a happy occasion—let's try not to involve lawyers," you may be saying. But whether or not you have fond feelings toward lawyers (or may even be about to marry one!), you should know the role the law will play in your marriage, which is, after all, an agreement between a man, a woman, and a state. (Except in Hawaii, where it may be between two men and the state or two women and the state. Or in Pennsylvania, where it's between a man, a woman, and the commonwealth. But that's a whole other book.)

Legal Benefits

The moment you're legally married, you'll go through a life's worth of legal changes, painlessly, invisibly, and probably without your even noticing. But it's worthwhile to note what they are: most of the changes are for the better. When's the last time the law worked for you?

The law of the land is merely *tolerant* of couples who live together, whereas it encourages and even rewards marriage, with the occasional exception made by the Internal Revenue Service. For example: before you marry, the legal relationship that exists between the two of you, even if you live together, is murky. If one of you should be knocked unconscious and need medical treatment, there may not even be legal grounds for one of you to authorize emergency surgery for the other.

After you marry, the first person that emergency workers turn to will be your spouse.

When buying a house, married couples can apply jointly for a loan and combine their incomes simply by virtue of the fact that they are married. Unmarried couples trying to accomplish the same thing run into much more flack.

If one of you obtains insurance from work, the other is almost always automatically covered under the policy *if you're married*. If you're not married, most companies are not willing to take on the burden of insuring a mere POSSLQ (Person of the Opposite Sex Sharing Living Quarters).

Legal Pitfalls

Several problems must be avoided. First of all, *make sure you're allowed to marry.* Sounds simple, doesn't it? But every year, hundreds of perfectly loving couples discover that even though they think they're married, they're not. This can happen if

• *One of you is still married to someone else.* If one of you was once married, that person must have the divorce finalized before the second marriage will be valid. If your first marriage took place in a big church with 1,000 guests, you'd know enough to realize that you have to have that divorce before the second marriage counts.

But there are those who are married and don't even know it. Common-law marriage is recognized in nine states plus the District of Columbia. This is a term for a legally sanctioned marriage that takes place without a formal ceremony or license, and no, you don't have to live together 7 years before such a legal state occurs. Each of the states that recognize common-law unions have their own rules, but in some locales, merely asking "Will you marry me?" and receiving a positive reply constitutes a legal marriage. Read that carefully: such a marriage is just as enforceable as the one you're about to plan. And once a common-law marriage exists and is recognized by one state, you're married in every other state as well until you get properly divorced. If you discover that one of you is already legally married to someone else, that marriage must be ended before this one will be legal.

• *You're not of legal age to marry.* Each state has its own laws, but if you're 18, you're legal everywhere. If you're under 18, check with the local Legal Aid Society or marriage bureau to see if you can legally marry in your state.

What Legal Hoops Must We Jump Through Before Our Wedding?

You should have an overview of what must happen before you can marry; the annals of wedding history are littered with the stories of couples who got to the church only to discover that they didn't have everything they needed to make the union legally valid.

A ceremony by a cleric is usually just icing on the cake and does not always guarantee a legal marriage; since laws vary state to state, you should inquire about the rules where you live. Typically, you must obtain a *marriage license.* It's a lot easier than getting a driver's license. A marriage license is more or less permission from the state to get married. Usually a fee is charged, and many states require that both partners have blood drawn to demonstrate that neither one of you has syphilis or rubella. In a handful of states, you must prove that you are free from AIDS (acquired immune deficiency syndrome) as well. Getting results for some of these blood tests takes 1 to 2 weeks, so don't plan to get your license the day before the wedding.

As mentioned above, if either of you has been married before, written proof of divorce must be proffered before a license can be issued. In a few states, there is a waiting period before obtaining a wedding license, or between issuance of the license and the wedding. Other states issue licenses that are valid for periods of time as short as 30 days, so it's crucial to time your visit to the courthouse so the license is still valid on the day you plan to marry.

Prenuptial Agreements

When you marry, the laws of the land will alter your relationship to your stuff. Some of your property will continue to be owned separately; other property will become joint property. The same is true of debts. What is individually owned and what is jointly owned is determined by the whim of the state where you live. In some places, creditors can dun either one of you for credit-card debt incurred by only one of you; in other places, they can't.

A prenuptial agreement has more to do with protecting both partners' possessions (or "covering your assets") than anything else. Typically, prenuptial agreements in movies and television are portrayed as a wicked document intended to allow a billionaire tycoon (who looks like Dr. Evil) to threaten to impoverish his beautiful (but poor) wife should she leave him. He's usually played by a snarling heavy, who growls at his beautiful little wife (played by someone like Lindsay Wagner), "If you leave me, you'll have *nothing!*" as he waves the prenuptial agreement in her face. In real life, there are plenty of practical reasons to consider a prenuptial agreement, even if you aren't Dr. Evil or Lindsay Wagner.

If either of you has a small business, a prenuptial agreement can help keep the finances of that enterprise separate from your household finances. Let's pretend that one of you co-owns a business selling batter-dipped deep-fried butter at state fairs. Further, let's pretend that this business has assets including 42 deep-fried butter carts and inventory of 6,000 pounds of butter, oil, and so on, all valued at around $82,000, co-owned by one of you and by a man whom we'll call Farmer Fred in a partnership.

Your pending marriage could complicate the batter-dipped deep-fried butter business, scaring Farmer Fred. "I like to know who I'm dealing with" has always been his motto. "And now that you're getting married, that spouse of yours—who seems like a good egg and all—might interfere with the business. Not saying that'll happen, but it might." If the business has been a success, there's no sense in scaring Farmer Fred, and a prenuptial agreement could record in writing that the business will be separately owned by the spouse who has always owned it.

Another type of prenuptial agreement takes the exact opposite tack: instead of keeping possessions separate, it explicitly mixes them together. This might help you get a home loan or car loan, for example.

If you do decide to enter into a prenuptial agreement, be sure to have separate lawyers represent each of you. This may sound like a doubling of expenses, but if you both use the same attorney, it could render the whole agreement invalid in some states.

Taxes

You know that little box on the tax return form that asks about whether you're single or married? The IRS isn't inquiring so that they can send you anniversary presents. They tax you differently depending on whether you're single or married. For some couples, the amount of tax paid actually goes up—what is called the "marriage penalty"—but the tax code is a Byzantine document prepared by legislators without regard to logic or consistency. Just be aware that it might be worthwhile to consult a tax advisor after getting married to see how your situation has changed. And as each new year brings new weird tax laws, you can see how tax advisors have real job security, year-in, year-out.

Death

You're going to die—I hope not before you've read this chapter (which will explain all the eternal mysteries of life and death in simple, declarative sentences), but rumor has it that some time or another, everyone's number comes up. It may seem odd to contemplate The Unhappy Inevitable while planning your wedding, but the fact is many marriage ceremonies include the phrase "until death do us part" or some variation on that theme.

The function of a will, like that of a prenuptial agreement, is primarily to sort out your stuff. Whether you own millions of dollars in stocks and bonds or just two really nice dogs and a quilt collection, you may want to make sure that your wishes as to what will happen to your things after your death are carried out. If you die without a will, the lawmakers down at the state capitol decide who gets which of your things.

Say it again: if you die without a will, the same people who designed the department of motor vehicles decide for you who gets your things. Pretty scary notion, considering these are also the *same sorts of people who created the tax code* and lunatic laws like "no spitting on Sunday," which still remain on the books. This is not to say that when you die the lawmakers will certainly do something crazy with your assets; it's just a very likely possibility. And who knows what kind of changes may occur between now and then.

But you can bypass the lawmakers by merely making out a

will, taking the decision-making power away from them. Do you want your spouse to inherit everything? Put it in writing and you can be assured it will happen. Leave it up to the whims of the legislature and your estate could wind up going to your third cousin once removed (the very same guy who wanted to come to your wedding but you couldn't figure out how he was related).

There are any number of ways to make a will. Some people like to use the "make a will yourself" kits that sell for about $50. These same kinds of people enjoy bungee jumping, riding motorcycles without a helmet, and eating raw hamburger that's been sitting in the sun. They might be okay, but they're still tempting fate. One wrong signature, one lack of notarization, and depending on which state you live in, your assets might wind up with wacko Cousin Floyd.

Go to a lawyer instead. You might end up paying $100 or more, but you'll have the peace of mind of knowing that your will is legal and properly drawn up, and your assets will go where they're intended to go.

Children

If your spouse-to-be has children, do you automatically become their mother (or father)? No, you do not. Natural parents have precedence under law, and no legal relationship exists between a stepparent and child unless further action is taken, such as an adoption.

How to Find a Good Family Lawyer

The best way to find a good family lawyer is to watch late-night television and see which lawyer wears the loudest clothes in a cheaply made commercial. If he says, "I will fight for you!", if she wears at least two different patterns of plaid simultaneously, if he has a crummy toupee, if she has an 800 number that spells her name, that's your lawyer. Oh, wait. Sorry. That's the *worst* way to pick a lawyer.

The best way is as follows:

1. Go by personal recommendation. The best recommendation you can have for a family attorney is the glowing testimonial of a satisfied client. Ask your friends, your family, and your boss if they know of a good family attorney. Try to ensure that your friends giving the recommendation got the same kind of legal advice you seek; an excellent entertainment attorney might make a terrible family lawyer.

2. If you can find no such glowing endorsement (we're talking about lawyers here, after all), call the local bar association, which may provide you with a list of lawyers specializing in family law. Or contact the American Bar Association, Family Law Section, whose members either practice family law exclusively or devote a large portion of their time to it.

3. If you need to narrow your search, you can find out how good a particular lawyer is by looking in the *Martindale-Hubbell Law Directory,* which rates lawyers the same way the Consumers Union rates cars (except there are still no crash tests for lawyers). The *Martindale-Hubbell Law Directory* should be in your local library.

4. Once you've selected a lawyer, make sure that he or she is working for you. Ask for a cost estimate up front. Ask how much experience the lawyer has had in similar matters. And ask for explanations of anything complicated or unfamiliar. You're paying good money to have things explained, not obfuscated.

Chapter 9

The
Honeymoon

AMERICAN STOCK PHOTOGRAPHY

*W*eddings require a lot of hard work as the two of you solve problems you've never had to deal with before and may never deal with again (until *your* children get married, but that's a whole different set of problems). As you plan and anticipate the big day, sometimes the love the two of you share can become temporarily obscured by your focus on really important subjects like whether you're justified in spending an extra $240 on the pink champagne or whether to have a disc jockey or a band play at the reception. Even when there are no conflicts between the two of you (most of the time, one hopes), it seems like others can make the path to the altar aggravating enough that some days you may wonder if it's all worth it. If frustrations are building, try this:

> *Close your eyes and imagine: Your wedding day is over.*
> *The ceremony was beautiful, moving, and memorable. Many friends*
> *and loved ones attended and witnessed the two of you exchanging*
> *wedding vows. The reception surpassed all expectations.*
>   *And now you're married.*

Hard as it may be to conceive of now (while you're making plans), one day your wedding will be over. And that's a great opportunity to spend some quality time together—without all those friends, family members, clergy, and everyone else hanging around. That's the time for your honeymoon to begin.

The anticipation of the honeymoon can do wonders for your attitude during the prewedding period. As you run yourselves ragged making arrangements and paying bills for seemingly everyone else in the world but yourselves, the promise of a honeymoon after the wedding is sweet. If the wedding is a nine-course meal, the honeymoon is dessert. A honeymoon isn't hard to plan, and it doesn't have to be expensive. The most important thing is to have a few days for yourselves after the hectic pace of the wedding. The time you spend together as newlyweds is more important than money spent or distance traveled to any resort.

Sometimes the demands of planning a wedding seem so enormous that working couples opt to take time off from their jobs *before* the wedding, leaving little time after. These people get married and must immediately return to the grind. Bad idea. If you have any control over the matter, try to save a few days or a week after the ceremony before you have to return to work. Your honeymoon is important because it gives you a chance to catch your breath after the wedding before plunging back into the daily routine.

What Is the Prime Objective of a Honeymoon?

Your honeymoon affords you some private time together to rest, to relax, and to have tons of sex. Fooling around, making whoopee, watching the submarine races, making love—call it what you will, it'll never be quite the same as in the first few days after getting married. If in addition to spending some "quality time" together you also take a fabulous cruise or a ski vacation or a trip to the Poconos, that's great, too . . . but don't let the vacation part interfere with the "being together" part. Something about pretty glossy ads in bridal magazines can lure couples to do things they'd never consider doing other-wise—like snowboarding or hot-air ballooning. That's fine; just don't forget to leave plenty of time for sex. And neither your parents nor your priest will raise an objection, either: you'll be married.

Where Should We Go?

If you've purchased enough bridal magazines, you probably have a pretty good idea of which vacation destinations consider themselves to be honeymoon worthy. Typically, such an advertisement shows a good-looking couple in bathing suits walking down a sandy beach and/or bathing in an oversized champagne glass. "Walking down a sandy beach" gets an *A* as far as romance, relaxation, and the promise of some good times together. "Bathing in a champagne glass" is simply absurd; it would never occur to anyone except perhaps the designer of a Las Vegas revue, and then in the context of a conga line, not as a vacation destination.

The point is that what the two of you might like to do after the wedding is a highly personal decision that may involve neither walking down the beach nor sitting in a champagne glass. What if you're both history buffs and would prefer a honeymoon visiting scenes of historic battles? What if you both like hiking and fishing? What if the one thing that the two of you want to do, more than anything in the whole world, is to visit the largest hydroelectric generating dam in North America? For some couples, all of these are excellent; you may share a passion that lends itself to a post-nuptial vacation. But just remember—*none of these vacation ideas will ever be advertised in a bridal magazine!*

You should begin planning your honeymoon by talking to each other (a good way to plan just about everything in life

*N*ot all honeymoon destinations are advertised in bridal magazines.

AMERICAN STOCK PHOTOGRAPHY

from this point on). Figure out how much time you'll have for a honeymoon, what you might like to do, and how much money you have to spend.

> *Ed and Lisa decided that their honeymoon should include everything they'd ever dreamed of experiencing on a vacation. They flew first class to Miami and from there took a cruise ship through the Caribbean, stopping at several fabulous island destinations. On their way home, they came through New Orleans and spent two nights in a beautiful hotel.*
>
> *What did they do during much of this entire fantasy vacation? They worried about how they were going to pay for it all.*
>
> *Before the wedding, each of them had applied for several credit cards. Inexperienced in the ways of easy credit, they didn't recognize the difference between "a $10,000 line of credit" and "$10,000 to blow."*
>
> *"I wish we'd stayed somewhere closer to home. First-class air travel cost an extra seven hundred dollars, for a two-hour plane trip," said Ed. "We did get free drinks and linen with our airplane food. But not seven hundred dollars' worth!"*
>
> *Lisa enjoyed the trip more than Ed but found that one Caribbean island is pretty much like any other. And the cruise ship was populated with rich people, most of whom were pretty old.*

Ed and Lisa saw ads featuring alluring couples walking in the sand and decided that looked pretty good. But they got carried away; with all the best intentions, they got in over their head and wound up with a fancier honeymoon than they really wanted or could afford. The lesson? Don't get in over your head; it can actually diminish the honeymooning experience.

> *Sue and Juan, from Portland, Oregon, met each other at a dinner party thrown by their mutual friend Keith. Needless to say, their story ends*

in their falling in love and becoming engaged. The problem was, as Sue put it, "Keith, who introduced us." Or, as Juan noted, "Keith was driving us up the wall." Both immediately added that they think Keith is a "great guy" who "gets credit for introducing us" but had some rather rigid ideas about how they should spend their honeymoon.

Specifically, he wanted them to use his time-share.

Back in the 1980s, Keith paid a huge amount of money for the right to spend 2 weeks a year in Fort Lauderdale, Florida. Juan and Sue's first choice for a honeymoon was to go to British Columbia, to do cross-country skiing and stay in a cozy little cabin. They told Keith, "Thank you for the kind offer, but we already have some plans." Then Keith offered to throw in airfare, and neither of them had the heart to tell him that they both hate hot weather, and even more, were repelled by the prospect of spending their honeymoon surrounded by drunken students on spring break.

So because they're both a little too shy and a little too polite (blame it on the Pacific Northwest), Juan and Sue spent their honeymoon in Florida, surrounded by sunburned, hungover college students. They had a great time anyway—in spite of everything—and it makes a great story for them to tell, but they still wish they'd fought for their dream vacation. The moral is that your honeymoon is your honeymoon. Only the two of you can decide what feels right—not your parents, not your friends, and certainly not Keith.

Talk to Each Other

Once you've gotten over the misunderstandings from other people, your next goal is to find a mutually satisfying honeymoon destination. The longer the period before your wedding that you have to discuss this, the more alternatives will remain viable.

Long before your wedding, send in the reader reply card from all the bridal magazines you have, as well as any travel magazine that caters to your preferred destinations. The hotels, tourist boards, and resorts that advertise will happily flood your mailbox with promotional literature. Bridal magazines can't possibly cover every possibility, so if the two of you share a special interest—for example, horseback riding, astronomy, or hydroelectric power—consider looking for honeymoon destinations in a specialty magazine. For more four-color flyers, visit a travel agent. Travel agents charge you no fee for their services; they are paid a set percentage by the airlines and resorts.

Once you've gotten many, many flyers, it's time to let the discussions begin. If you're in the right mood, every place in every brochure looks romantic. One nice thing about marriage is that you'll have your whole life together to visit all the places that you don't choose for your honeymoon.

But the question remains now: How do you weed out the bad ones?

- Don't confuse a nice brochure with a nice destination. It is much more common to find a good-looking photograph of a crummy resort than the other way around. A good photographer is a lot cheaper than a remodeling job.
- If you're traveling far away, make sure the weather in the picture is the same as the weather when you'll be visiting. You'd be surprised how many people find that the first day of their vacation is spent buying warmer clothes.

Your Honeymoon Budget

The prices quoted in brochures can vary widely, and sometimes the "low" one proves more expensive than the "high" one because the latter includes amenities like meals or a

$\mathscr{D}$istinctively colored luggage that is identifiable from a distance is useful if your honeymoon takes you through Denver.

AMERICAN STOCK PHOTOGRAPHY

rental car that are not included in the low one. When you're evaluating which honeymoon offers a better value, make sure that you compare similarly configured trips. Be sure that you account for all of the following costs:

- *Travel.* Whether by train, plane, or automobile, you have to get from here to there. Some trips include the airfare; others expect you to pay airfare on top of their other fees.
- *Meals.* Some resorts include all meals; others, only breakfast; some, no meals at all.
- *Taxes.* Sales tax in some places goes up to 10 percent, and some special "room taxes" imposed by cities can add another 15 percent after that. Suddenly an "$80-a-night" room costs $100. Ask about the tax rate when booking.
- *Gratuities.* In some foreign countries, it is customary to tack on a service charge of up to 15 percent. Ask if this is included in the price quoted.
- *Entertainment.* What, exactly, are you going to be doing when you're not having sex? Are sports, day trips, museums, or other entertainment included in the package cost? If not, how much will they add to the cost of your honeymoon?
- *Extra charges.* What extra charges will you incur? Are local telephone calls free, or $2 a call? (It does happen!)
- *Per person or per room.* Is the published price per person or per room?
- *Noise level and aesthetics.* How quiet is this destination? You don't want to spend your first few days of marriage overlooking a construction site or a freeway. A beautiful photograph of a building can hide the fact that it sits atop a subway.
- *Room categories.* How many classes of rooms are there? Any price that begins with *from,* as in *rooms from $1.50 per night,* means that you'll never get that price. Also, the room in the brochure is inevitably the superfabulous suite; ask if it's

$\mathcal{D}$on't forget to take pictures.

AMERICAN STOCK PHOTOGRAPHY

similar to the one you'll be staying in. Package tours occasionally are able to offer a low rate by putting their customers in the crummiest rooms.

• *Goodies*. Are there any freebies? See if your destination tosses in bonuses like a free happy hour, a fruit basket, or a VCR and videotapes.

• *Convenience*. Ask if there's room service or a restaurant in the hotel. It's no fun to have to drive somewhere for every meal.

Use the honeymoon budget form below to compare your favorite destinations. If some destinations include sports, entertainment, or meals, they may be less expensive than they appear.

Honeymoon Budget

$_____ Travel for two (round trip)

$_____ Car rental

$_____ Gasoline

$_____ Hotel room including tax and gratuity (___ days × $_____ per day)

$_____ Breakfasts (___ days × $_____ per day)

$_____ Lunches (___ days × $_____ per day)

$_____ Dinners (___ days × $_____ per day)

$_____ Entertainment

$_____ Spending cash (___ days × $_____ per day)

$_____ Sales tax

$_____ Gratuities

$_____ **Total**

The "Almost Free" Honeymoon

Is the discussion of travel depressing you as you realize that it's just all too expensive? Don't worry about it. The point of a honeymoon isn't to *go* somewhere together . . . it's to *be* somewhere together. And that somewhere can be your own home or apartment. Your challenge changes from getting away from all distractions into keeping all distractions away. This may require a little bit of subterfuge on your part . . . which is good practice for when you are married.

First, begin your disinformation campaign well in advance. Keep secret that the two of you are going to spend the first few days of married bliss at home. Instead, drop a series of hints that communicate two points—first, that you're keeping your destination secret, and second (this is the subterfuge part), that it's far, far away. This fake destination should be fairly convincing; you might even get a travel book or a few brochures and let someone "accidentally" figure out where you're going.

On the day of the wedding, be sure that both of you have suitcases packed and ready to go. Anyone who sees them will have no doubts that you're going away.

A few days before the wedding, you need to fill your apartment or house with all that's needed for a romantic few days together. Get candles, massage oil, and the other tools of romance. Make sure you have plenty of supplies, including romantic food—fruit, wine, chocolate, the meal you ate when you first got engaged. Reserve rentals of the most romantic movies ever made, and also a few movies you actually want to watch. (Sometimes a comedy or action picture is a nice break from the unrelenting romance.)

On the big day, when you're leaving the reception, make sure you aren't followed. If a friend is driving for you (or if you have a taxi or limousine), make sure that person is sworn to secrecy. As you leave, make sure everyone sees your suitcases go into the car. Take a circuitous route around the city until you're sure you haven't been followed. Then go home. Hide the car. Pull down the curtains. Unplug the telephone. Light the candles. And begin your married life right.

Chapter 10

Moving in Together

AMERICAN STOCK PHOTOGRAPHY

*A*lthough there's no doubt getting married is a serious commitment, many of the preparations seem less appropriate to an event that will change your life forever and more like planning a really, really big party. If you screw something up, it's not the end of the world: the rehearsal dinner, the ceremony itself, the reception, and the honeymoon all come quickly to an end. If one of you is obsessed with having the band play selections from *Camelot* and the other lukewarm about show tunes, it's easy enough to give in—play it! It's just a song.

The real test of compatibility comes when you pit yourselves against something more permanent . . . like moving in together. Since the first years of your marriage will probably be spent wherever you first move (unless you're already living together), it pays a high "happiness dividend" if you select that first home *carefully*. Don't assume on the basis of your compatibility in so many other areas that you'll have the same taste in housing. A few hours figuring out your individual and mutual likes and dislikes can save weeks of hunting for an apartment or house and provide years of good living.

Buy or Rent?

Some real estate agents assert that if you can afford to do so, it's better to buy than rent. "You build equity," goes the realtor's argument, "and then there's the many tax benefits—for example, mortgage interest is deductible!" But then again, they're real estate agents, aren't they, and what would you expect them to say on the subject?*

Property ownership's a swell thing, and *if* you can afford it and *if* you're sure you won't move again in the next couple of years and *if* you really love a particular home in a particular neighborhood . . . then buying really is better than renting. But you're already making a lot of changes in your lives. Sometimes, no matter how carefully a newlywed couple plans ahead, they pick a place to live that doesn't quite work out. Maybe it's a little too small, maybe it's too hot or too cold, maybe it's too far from family, from work, or from friends. If you buy, you may be stuck there a little longer than antici-pated. A better plan is to use the first year of marriage to get used to each other and learn each other's tastes and habits before you commit irrevocably to a house, condo, or co-op.

And those tax savings you hear so much about? Well, they "save" you money in much the same way as a "20 percent off" sale: to "save" $40 in taxes, you might have to spend $200; with mortgage payments, to "save" $200, you have to spend $1,000.

If You Immediately Buy a House Anyway

You're confident that everything's going to work out and you're the kind of decisive, happening couple that is the envy of all of us less-decisive souls in the world who like to take things one major life decision at a time. But here's a cautionary

---

*Author's note: almost everyone in the author's family is *in* the real estate busi-ness and the author knows he'll be tweaked for making any cracks about the many benefits of home ownership. It paid for his college, after all, as well as 18 years' worth of room and board. Therefore, if you're a blood relative, you might skip the next couple of paragraphs.

tale, followed by some advice on how to make the simultaneous transition into your new marriage and new home easier.

"Mr. X" and "Mrs. X" (their real names) live in a major metropolitan area known for its earthquakes, riots, and police beatings. During their engagement, they found the home of their dreams. Well, not *their* dreams, exactly, but someone's dreams: it had a pretty yard, sunny living quarters, and a detached garage that would make Mr. X a nice home office and was on the market at a price they could comfortably afford. The low price made it easy to overlook the graffiti and bullet hole–riddled walls that made their dream house indistinguishable from what you or I might call a crack house or gangbangers' lair. If you watch *America's Most Wanted* or *Cops,* you may have seen their house, more than once. But they were in love, and they bought it anyway.

After they married, the Xes were able to turn their newlyweds' crack house into a stylish home with lots of love, paint, sweat equity, dedication, and the assistance of some overpaid contractors. They expressed one regret: both wished they had waited an extra month before moving in, as all the work took much longer to do once they were living there. The moral may be "Fix up the fixer-upper before moving in," or the moral may be simply "Don't buy a crack house, no matter how low the price."

Whether you buy or rent and whether you choose an apartment or house, you still have many decisions ahead of you. Shopping for your first marital address can actually be fun. Remember always that your home is both a place to be and a place to do things. No matter how charming a potential home *appears,* it must still fit into your lives, or you'll have some regrets. Make your house or apartment fit your lives; don't fit your lives to your house or apartment.

Some people approach the problem of home selection logically and sensibly, comparing all contenders in terms of price, square footage, amenities, and comparable neighborhood value, balancing each trait against all the others in a scientifically designed spreadsheet that assigns a numerical score to each home; then they simply pick the place with the highest score and move in. Then, a few years later, the midlife crisis; then, the feeling late in life that maybe they should have been a little more whimsical when they were young.

You don't even want to meet those kinds of "sensible" people. Rumor has it they are colluding with the pod people from Andromeda and are set on taking over the earth.

Sensible decision making is overrated, and on top of that, it's no fun. Picking your newlywed home isn't strictly a logical activity, anyway. We all live our lives differently, and choosing a place that makes a subjective good fit is far more important than picking a home that someone else approves of. Additionally, you get to head off the midlife crisis, the alien collusion, and all the rest of it.

An excellent way to discover where your personal tastes lay is the completely unscientific "let's pretend" style of home selection. You remember what "let's pretend" is, don't you? You did it back when you were 10.

Let's Pretend

Walk through each potential home, together, and separately, imagining yourselves doing the things you genuinely like to do. If cooking appeals to you, stand in the kitchen and pretend to cook the meal you make most often; where will you set down the pots and pans? Where will you mash the potatoes? Where will you force-feed the goose (for that really fresh pâté)?

If you while away many a pleasant hour watching television (and who doesn't?), it's imperative you determine, using the "let's pretend" method, where the TV goes, where the two of you sit, and where everything else in the room is supposed to go. Many people, while home hunting, neglect to consider the question of TV viewing and then the TV winds up in the bedroom. Bad idea. *You'll be newlyweds.* You want to be in the bedroom, but not watching the tube (nudge-nudge, wink-wink).

"Let's pretend" will reveal the benefits and inadequacies of potential homes at the same time it teaches you about each other's values. As you walk through homes, imagining yourselves doing the things you like to do, listen carefully to each other's concerns. Test-driving a home can help a couple iron out many problems before they have the chance to *become* problems.

Some living arrangements provide special problems that require some discussion to sort out. First among these is if one of you moves into the other's preexisting home. One of you gives up your current living situation and moves all your stuff into the other's place. Seems like a great idea, but remember: the person who lived there already has to allow the one moving in to exert some influence over the living space.

Paul and Henrietta got married; she moved from her parents' home into Paul's two-bedroom, one-bath apartment. In the weeks before she moved in, Henrietta imagined all the changes she would work on Paul's apartment, to turn it from a charming-but-boyish bachelor pad into a swell first home for a married couple. She wanted to replace some of the movie posters with her own art prints (bye-bye, *Pulp Fiction;* hello, Renoir.) She envisioned hanging her pots and pans over the sink in the kitchen (and taking down the beer-bottle collection.) In short, she had her motor running to do a Martha Stewart–ish makeover.

In Paul's mind, the only difference after Henrietta moved in would be that Henrietta lived there. When she started taking

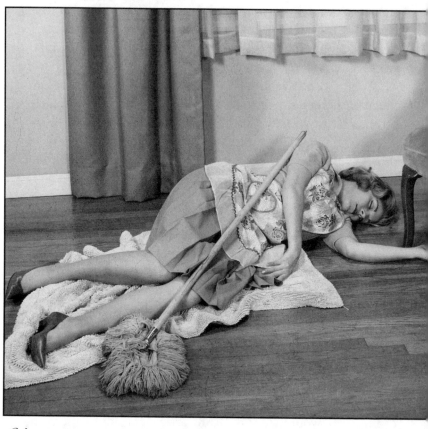

$\mathcal{Y}$ou may soon discover that one of you takes domestic order more seriously than the other does.

AMERICAN STOCK PHOTOGRAPHY

down the movie posters, he complained. ("I've memorized every one of Samuel Jackson's lines!—'The Big Kahuna burger. That is a tasty burger!'") But when he came home to discover that the carefully assembled beer-bottle collection ("42 states and 9 foreign countries are represented") had been sent to the recycling station, he hit the roof. And she hit the roof.

Who was right? Even Judge Wapner himself couldn't decide who was to blame—because both of them were: Henrietta, for decorating without asking, and Paul, for assuming that he could assert territorial rights simply because he lived in the apartment first.

The lesson is this: when one newlywed moves into the other's preexisting apartment, a long discussion should take place about how both can have a stake in its appearance.

Another special case occurs when one spouse is moving to another's town. Often times, young lovers meet at college or while on vacation and get engaged to be married. If they come from different towns, the decision of where to live can be a tough one. It's especially hard if only one of the spouses-to-be is shopping for a place to live.

Jane and Dick (no relation to Dick and Jane) met at Northwestern University, fell in love, and decided to get married. Because of favorable job opportunities, they decided to relocate to Des Moines, but Jane moved a couple months in advance of Dick to scout possible homes. Because she wanted Dick's opinion of each house, she took photos of the homes she considered, then mailed them back to Chicago.

Thanks to the twin nineteenth-century miracles of photography and telephony, they were able to discuss the merits and shortcomings of each potential abode while located hundreds of miles apart. That's because Jane was a very clever photographer. Rather than stand back and take a single photograph of each room, she created photo montages. Here's how you can do the same: standing in one spot, preferably near the center of a room, turn so that the left edge of the camera viewfinder is lined up with the left edge of the room. Snap a picture; then, pivoting on the same point, move your head to the right. Keeping your camera viewfinder on the same level, move until the left edge of the viewfinder is now where the right edge previously was. Repeat until you have photographed the entire room, then move on to the next room. Do the same for any outside walls if it is a house and for any public areas if you are considering an apartment complex.

After you develop the pictures, carefully tape them together in file folders so that you now have a complete record of every room. Not only is this useful if you are far away from each other, but it also can be used to compare two contenders. Especially when looking at a large number of homes, since they can run together in the mind. Comparing photographs side by side will jog the memory and make decision making easier.

A similar way to compare homes is by videotaping them. Just be sure to videotape every view and every angle. One caveat, however: if you videotape several potential homes, it can be hard to continually fast-forward and rewind the videotape to find the one you want. So although photographs are a little more work up front, they are easier to use later on.

What's It Going to Cost?

Everyone wants to pay the least amount for the best possible apartment (or house), but sometimes it feels like comparing apples and oranges. Take two apartments, one $100 a month more expensive than the other. The expensive apartment is in a slightly better neighborhood and is closer to your jobs; the cheaper one is further from work and in a slightly worse neighborhood but includes utilities and a two-car garage. Which is a better deal?

You have to take all the costs into account. These include the following:

- *Rent.* Duh.
- *Utilities.* How much per month will you save by having the landlord pay utilities?
- *Insurance.* This is a tricky one, because insurance costs sometimes differ between neighborhoods. For home and auto insurance, insurers often tie the cost to the ZIP code of the area. Ask in advance. Saving $50 in rent isn't a big deal if you pay it back out again in auto and home insurance.
- *Driving.* The cost to operate an automobile is around 35¢ a mile. A 15-mile commute costs $210 a month, not including the time you spend in traffic.
- *Other fees.* All condominiums charge a monthly fee on top of the monthly payment. Some areas charge for garbage pickup, whereas others do not.

COST COMPARISON FORM		
	Abode #1	*Abode #2*
Rent (or mortgage payment)	$_____	$_____
Utilities	$_____	$_____
Insurance	$_____	$_____
Auto mileage	$_____	$_____
Other fees	$_____	$_____
Total	$_____	$_____

How Much Is Too Much?

The usual rule of thumb is that the amount you spend for housing should not exceed a third of your combined take-home pay. Take-home pay is the amount left over after all taxes have been withheld—the amount you actually get to deposit in the bank.

Tips for Apartment and House Hunting

Here are some things you should definitely check out before you plunk down money.

1. Check the water pressure. No matter how nice everything else is, if you sign a 1-year lease (or take out a 30-year mortgage) and then learn you'll have dribbly showers all that time, you'll be kicking yourselves.

2. If you'll be renting, find out if there are any limits to how much the rent can be raised, and how often. Some unscrupulous landlords lure tenants in with easy, low rents for the first 6 months and then hit them with a big increase once they've settled in. See if your area has any rent controls.

3. Read your lease carefully and negotiate any points you disagree with. Sometimes restrictions are put in standard preprinted forms that a landlord will be happy to waive. Typical examples include a prohibition on overnight guests.

4. Don't be pressured into signing a lease until you're comfortable with the terms and the apartment. A typical high-pressure tactic is to refer to the tenant who's going to take the apartment unless you sign the lease right now. Don't do it.

5. Visit the potential home at odd times of day. Sometimes a place that seems charming at noon may be terrifying at midnight.

6. In addition to choosing a home, you're also choosing a neighborhood. Find out how far the place under consideration is from the nearest grocery, gas station, pharmacy, and so on.

7. On a rental, find out the total move-in cost. Cleaning deposit, key deposit, security deposit, and first and last months' rent can add up. Ask what will be refunded should you move out.

$\mathcal{B}$e sure to check the water pressure before signing a lease. It also helps to actually look at the apartment before making a decision.

AMERICAN STOCK PHOTOGRAPHY

Change-of-Address Checklist

If one or both of you will undergo a name change, note that on any change-of-address cards. Preprinted change-of-address cards can be obtained free from the U.S. Postal Service and should be sent to the following:

- ♀ Your current employers
- ♀ Your previous employers (for tax forms)
- ♀ Magazines for which you have subscriptions
- ♀ Banks—checking accounts, savings accounts, certificates of deposit (CDs), individual retirement accounts (IRAs), and so on
- ♀ Credit card issuers
- ♀ Places of worship
- ♀ College alumni associations
- ♀ High-school alumni associations
- ♀ Families
- ♀ Friends
- ♀ Libraries where you hold patron cards
- ♀ Doctors and dentists
- ♀ Utility companies with whom you already have accounts
- ♀ Draft Registration Board (required for men between the ages of 18 and 25)
- ♀ Department of Motor Vehicles—driver's licenses, boat and trailer registrations, motorcycle registrations, car and truck registrations, and so forth
- ♀ Insurance companies (life, vehicle, and residence)
- ♀ State income tax board
- ♀ Internal Revenue Service

- ♥ Voter registration department of your county
- ♥ Social Security Administration (if your names are changing)
- ♥ School district (if either of you has children)
- ♥ Your local postmaster
- ♥ Veterinarians

Chapter 11

Second Thoughts, Why They're a Good Thing, and What to Do with Them

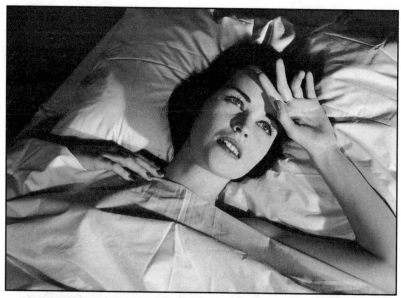

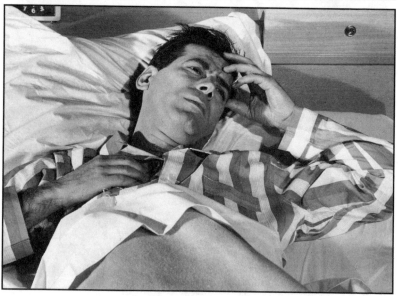

AMERICAN STOCK PHOTOGRAPHY

*T*he road to marriage isn't all parties and shopping; there's also a substantial amount of terrifying self-examination involved. Something about a marriage feels more permanent than anything you've ever done. So . . . *irrevocable.* Most wedding ceremonies include a shocking dose of unpleasant speculation—you know, the part that goes "in sickness and in health," that part where they say "for richer or for poorer," and most of all, that chilling phrase "till death do us part." Death? Unless you already have a terminal disease, that can seem a long, long way off. "You're asking me to commit right up to the point where I shuffle off this mortal coil?" you ask in astonishment. "That's a big commitment." Longer than a 30-year mortgage and more legally binding than going steady.

That can be pretty scary; that can give you cold feet.

But if you're serious about what you're getting into, don't be surprised if you start questioning the nature of the commitment you're going to make: "Forever? I'm supposed to stand in front of everyone I know and promise that I'll be with this person (whom I love a great deal) forever?" Your inner romantic might be ready and willing, but your inner lawyer will start carving out exceptions, kind of like those 10-page insurance contracts. "Till death do us part, *except in the occasion of War, Natural Disaster, Acts of God, or Force Majeure as defined in paragraph 2a below. This agreement subject to change without notice, and any element of this marriage that shall be determined to be unlawful shall not invalidate any other provision . . .*"

Forget it. There are no exceptions.

The simple words of the marriage ceremony are absolutes. It's an agreement between people of honor, the kind of agreement that citizens made in the days before attorneys' small print proliferated like so much paranoid graffiti, covering every product, grocery receipt, parking stub, and movie ticket. Marriage has no small print. It's absolute. Period. The end.

You will never be able to predict with any accuracy what the two of you will come up against. In this age of exceptions and exclusions, it's gratifying to encounter vows that are so permanent. No wiggle room. No ifs, ands, or buts. That's the power of marriage; that's its charm; but that's also why it's so scary.

If marriage's permanence is giving you a case of cold feet, don't worry. You're not the first couple to have second thoughts, and besides, doubts are not the end of the love affair so much as they are a sign that you're seriously considering what you're about to do.

"How can I make a promise that lasts forever when I don't know what will happen next year—or even next month?" That's a question that the inner lawyer—the one who wants certainty and guarantees and warranties—keeps asking. Tell the inner lawyer to take a well-deserved vacation and listen to the little quiet voice that knows the value of a leap into the unknown. That part of you already realizes that the impermanence and mutability of the world ("How can I know what's going to happen next month?") isn't an obstacle to marriage but rather a reason to tie the knot. You're promising to share your lives no matter what happens. You're promising that no matter who's president, no matter what the weather is, no matter if there's a war or a flood or an earthquake, no matter who wins the World Series, what's on TV, what you do for a living, how much the Dow Jones industrial average goes up or down, and no matter where you live or how much money you make, you still have each other.

The world's going to be a chaotic and unpredictable place whether or not you get married. The question to ask is if you want to face that chaotic, unpredictable place we call Earth by yourself or side by side with someone you love, and who loves you.

Even knowing all that you still have doubts and questions rattling around in your brain at 3 A.M. Questions like these:

• *Since statistics say that so many marriages end in divorce, why get married in the first place?*

People who cite this as a reason not to get married are hopeless dweebs, nearly beneath your contempt. First of all, a majority of marriages do *not* end in divorce. The straight-up statistical truth of the matter is squarely on the side of "go for it." But the bigger problem with this particular objection is allowing *statistics* to play any part in what remains a highly personal and individual decision. Would you refuse to buy a pair of shoes that fit you because *statistically* they won't fit most other people? Did numbers and averages play any part in falling in love? Was mathematical certainty a factor in deciding to exchange vows? Of course not. So next time someone suggests that the odds are against you, tell them that you're not playing the odds. You're getting married. That'll shut 'em up.

• *Our friends don't get along.*

It would be highly unusual if your friends *did* get along. Fortunately, it's not your friends who are getting married, so who cares?

Perhaps the roots of this sort of trepidation grow out of the fear that marriage may cut you off from your friends. If that's the case, talk about it. The vows don't read "love, honor, cherish, and break off all ties with the outside world." (Those would be the vows you take when joining a suicide cult.) After your wedding, you'll each keep some friends that the other finds disagreeable. That keeps life interesting and slightly off balance.

Take the case of Betsy and A.J.: they're both twenty-six years old and very much in love with each other; they are scheduled to get married, and they share many, many interests. They both like roller-blading; both are Methodists; they both like to stay up late watching old movies on television. They don't agree on everything—for example, Betsy's a Mac person and A.J. loves his Packard Bell computer—but they're so in love that each is prepared to dabble in foreign computer systems to make the marriage work.

No, their big obstacle is that Betsy has a few friends that A.J. doesn't like, and A.J. has a few friends that drive Betsy insane.

For example, take A.J.'s childhood friend Chad. A.J. always says, "Chad's a great guy," and quite a few people agree with him. Betsy, however, does not number among them. A.J. and Chad have experienced many great adventures together, like the eighth-grade camping trip when they had 22 inches of snow fall on their tent, the trading-card business they ran for two summers in junior high, the bike trips they took, and more recently, the time they went to the Metallica concert. Well, actually, a lot of Metallica concerts. Seventeen of 'em, and counting.

And although A.J. attended community college, earned a degree in restaurant management and now manages a pretty upscale restaurant, not to mention that he lives in an apartment of his own, his friend Chad kind of stagnated.

Stagnated is actually Betsy's word. A.J. likes to say that Chad "stayed true to his beliefs," even if his beliefs seem to consist mostly of *Miami Vice* reruns, any beer that costs less than $5 for 12 cans, and the musical stylings of the aforementioned rock combo. Chad also stayed true to his beliefs by letting his hair grow down to his butt and by continuing to wear the T-shirts that used to fit.

When A.J. got engaged to Betsy, he felt certain that eventually Betsy would come to appreciate his best friend's inner beauty. He wanted A.J. and Betsy to get along, and more important, to approve of each other. Unfortunately, one visit to Chad's basement home ("The Lair," he called it) and she had her doubts about Chad and, by extension, about A.J. It went about as well as giving a cat a bath.

After that visit, Betsy didn't really want her hubby hanging out a couple nights a month with Chad, and she never hesitated to say so. A.J.'s honor impugned, he defended Chad vociferously and chided Betsy for saying one word about him.

That's when they both got cold feet.

Who's wrong, A.J. or Betsy? Both of 'em.

Garth Brooks pointed out that it's perfectly all right to have friends in low places. But A.J. shouldn't impose his friends on Betsy. Conversely, she's within her rights to boycott The Lair, but she cannot expect A.J. to follow her lead.

And this all goes without mentioning some of Betsy's friends, like beauticians Trini and Lois, who are obsessed with doing a "makeover" on A.J., or May the Mumbler.

The bottom line is that you're marrying the person you're marrying, not their friends. And those friends, no matter how much you may object to them, helped make your fiancé (or fiancée) the man or woman that you fell in love with. It's all part of the package. Don't let it throw you off the course to the altar.

- *How come it feels like things are moving so fast?*

A lot of prewedding fears grow out of the many things that occur simultaneously around you while getting ready to get married. Besides getting married, you may be inviting out-of-town guests, reflecting on your past, contemplating your future, meeting strangers in your future spouse's family, taking time off from work or school, moving, and being at the center of attention for a while.

Gary and Brenda were both quiet, retiring sorts, who actually met in a library reading group, hit it off during a long discussion about John Le Carré, and got engaged a few months later. Their life plan was to be quiet and retiring *together*. So far, so good. But both are from large families and wanted to share their vows with family and friends. About a month before the wedding, Gary was at Brenda's apartment; they had intended to spend a quiet evening together and perhaps discuss a revisionist history of Prohibition that they'd both read. They neither read nor discussed a revisionist history of anything; instead, Brenda's telephone rang 17 times, mostly people asking about the wedding. The usually polite woman began answering the phone with an agitated "What?" instead of her usual "hello."

By the end of the night, Brenda and Gary had a little spat. What started as a little argument soon became a broad indictment of everything having to do with the wedding so far, and when Gary left, Brenda was in tears. The next call she made was to her mother; she said wasn't sure she wanted to get married after all.

The next day, she and Gary made up, and they learned an important lesson: love is romantic. Marriage is romantic. Getting married, though, sometimes feels like one enormous pain.

The *process* of getting married is a hassle, just like the *process* of getting a driver's license. Once you get that license, though, you never think back to driver's education class or the gory "blood on the pavement" movies, the mystery of the stick shift, or the lines down at the Department of Motor Vehicles. No, those problems are left behind the moment you're on the open road.

Similarly, the hoops you have to jump through to get married will be forgotten soon enough. Some wedding planning is just plain old boring work, but as long as you focus on the goal, you won't be overwhelmed by petty problems. No matter what unusual situations you find yourself in, remember: you only have to go through this once.

- *Why does it seem so fun to be single? (now that I'm about to get married)?*

A strange thing seems to happen beginning the day you get engaged. Suddenly, it seems like all the single people you know are throwing terrific parties and going on exciting outings to places you can't go because you're too busy planning a wedding—parties, concerts, trips. They're getting in shape down at the gym, they're getting promotions at work, and it's all because they're single!

Well, it's no secret that this is an illusion. Your mind has all kinds of clever ways to express anxiety, and a classic is the "life's greener on the other side of the fence" trick. Even if your single friends are really leading such exciting lives of adventure, it's because they are trying to distract themselves from the sad truth that they don't have love. Whether they're out climbing Mount Everest or hanging with top celebrities in New York City, the truth is they'd rather be planning a wedding of their own. They're probably looking back at you two, thinking of all the fun *you'll* be having with your wedding.

That's a rational explanation, but because fears and cold feet are irrational, they probably won't go away so easily. If you see a gang of single people dressed up to go out dancing, some part in the back of your mind is going to wish you were going with them. Nostalgia is a powerful force, and that's not nostalgia for 50 years ago; when you're suffering from cold feet, you can be nostalgic for the week before last.

Soak it up. You may miss your days as part of the singles scene, but that doesn't mean you have to relive them. From the safe perch of memory, it may seem like dating and being single are "fun," but that's just not the truth. It's a living hell of missed phone calls and "What should I wear?" and "Is my date staring at my zit?" and "Does s/he really like me?" and "You're sleeping with everyone that your partner has slept with." *Yuk. Gross.* Being married is so much better than that. Remember: you found love. That's what all those singles are out there looking for. The dirty secret of the singles set is that they'd trade places with either of you in a New York second.

Chapter 12

How Your Life Will Change— And It Will

$\mathcal{G}$etting married will change your lives. Not just in some grand poetic shot-by-Cupid's-arrow way, but rather in a number of distinct, measurable differences you will notice once you stop living life as two single individuals and begin living it as one married couple. These include legal changes, social changes, and some changes in the way you lead your day-to-day life.

Legal Changes

Because a marriage is an agreement between two people and the state, you need to deal with some of the legal ramifications of your upcoming marriage. One of the most obvious is the possibility that one or both of you will change your names.

Traditionally in this country, the bride takes on the surname of the groom, but as with most traditions, this practice is nowhere near as absolute and universal as it once was (though it remains the most common name change that occurs as a result of a marriage). An example is that if Mary Johansen married Robert Rasputin, she would change her name to Mary Rasputin.

Hyphenated names, in which the bride—or both bride and groom—take on both names is becoming more common; for example, Mary becomes Mary Johansen-Rasputin and/or Robert becomes Robert Rasputin-Johansen.

Many Spanish-speaking countries automatically allow the bride to retain her maiden name, by adding it *after* the groom's name. Thus, if our example couple were Costa Ricans, she would become Mary Rasputin Johansen. (Or more likely *Maria* Rasputin Johansen.) Their children (if they have any) keep both names in the same order as the bride, though their last names are alphabetized by the father's name—Baby Rasputin Johansen would sit in the R section of homeroom, not the J section.

Still one more possible name change occurs when both bride and groom abandon their original last names and take on a new, exotic blended last name. Our example couple might become Mary and Robert Rasjansen, or Mary and Robert Jansputin. Naturally, this kind of thing happens a lot more in places like New York City and California, but it is increasingly an option that couples are taking.

Regardless of *what* name change occurs as a result of your union, the world must be notified. "The world" in this case includes a list of some of the least-popular bureaucracies:

- Your state bureau of motor vehicles (for your vehicle registration and driver's license)
- Your employers' human resources department
- The Social Security Administration
- The Internal Revenue Service
- Your state income tax board
- Your county's voter registration service
- The State Department (if you have a passport)
- Credit-card issuers
- Insurance companies
- Banks and savings and loans
- Any schools or universities, if you're still in school, or their alumni associations if you're not—or if either of you has children attending school

Financial Changes

Right now, you may each have a checking account. After you marry, will you

A. Have one bank account to share?
B. Have two separate accounts, just like now?
C. Have three bank accounts—two separate and one that you share?

Think carefully before you answer. This question will be on the test, you are being graded, and spelling counts. Whatever decision you make is yours alone, but the author strongly recommends B or C—anything but a single joint account. Sure, you'll pay a little extra in bank fees, but there are very good reasons to keep separate accounts, beginning with an important factoid: most marital arguments are about money.

Let's say it again: most marital arguments are about money.

No matter what happens on sitcoms, in which everyone has plenty of dough and argues about everything *but* money, in real life, money is the source of most bickering. Since you know that, you can take an easy preemptive step to avoid some of those potential fights by maintaining separate accounts. You may believe sincerely that you'll be careful with the joint account but the day will come when both of you write checks without remembering to tell the other. It will happen. At the very best, that day (or more likely, days) will be unpleasant, and at the worst, it'll be an argument, along the lines of "It's your fault we bounced a check," followed shortly by "No, it's your fault we bounced a check" (repeat as necessary). Who wants those kinds of pointless discussions when you could be discussing philosophy, art, or *Gilligan's Island* or even having sex instead of arguing?

If this isn't going to dissuade you from keeping separate

accounts, by all means do what you need to do but don't forget that there is nothing romantic about those two little words *insufficient funds*. The fragile flower that will be your new marriage doesn't need the aggravation.

Insurance

Now that you're both about to join the club we can let you in on the biggest marital secret of all: lower insurance rates.

When was the last time you heard of an insurance company voluntarily *lowering* its rates? Maybe never. But the fact remains that married people live longer, get sick less often, take better care of themselves, and have fewer car accidents. Sounds like a pretty good deal even before you throw in the financial savings that come in the form of lowered insurance rates. So make sure that your insurance agent is alerted to the fact that you'll be marrying.

Holidays

Whether you celebrate Christmas, Ramadan, Yom Kippur, Kwanzaa, or just the Fourth of July and St. Patrick's Day, chances are each of you has a particular favorite way to spend each holiday. Maybe one of you "always" goes to a family picnic on Memorial Day and the other "always" gets together with friends to watch the Indy 500. Let's have another pop quiz (and yes, it's going to be on the final). What do you do?

A. Go your separate ways
B. Try to do both—a predawn picnic followed by car racing later in the day
C. Alternate years—picnic on odd years, Indy 500 on even years
D. Argue about it so much you wind up doing neither

If you don't plan ahead, there is a good chance you'll wind up with the "let's make each other miserable" option, D. And that's no fun.

Because the way we spend holidays is highly personal and filled with emotional associations, it sometimes feels traumatic to change the way we celebrate them. As you begin the new phase of your life—as a married couple—discuss candidly how you want to celebrate various holidays. Sometimes it's hard to break a holiday tradition, but it may be even harder to continue the tradition alone without your new spouse (who is attending another equally immutable traditional family gathering). The "try to do both" option is something many newlywed couples try, with mixed results. "We'll have Thanksgiving early in the day at his family's house, and late in the day at her family's house." This sounds like a good idea in concept, but in practice, it may involve lots of crazed racing from house to house, followed by overeating. A better solution may be to alternate years or even to alternate holidays; for example, "If we spend Thanksgiving with *his* family, then we will go to *her* family's house at Christmas [or Hanukkah, or Ramadan or Kwanzaa or whichever holiday you celebrate]."

Making Decisions Together

When you visit couples who have been happily married a long time, they sometimes give the impression that they agree on everything and that when they have to make a decision, large or small, they both automatically agree. Sometimes, when you meet such couples, it appears that one could speak for both of them; that they've synchronized their lives in a way that mere mortals can only imagine.

It's an illusion.

Even couples married 50 years don't agree on everything;

and they don't even *have to* agree on much to still have a happy, productive life as a married couple. The illusion that they agree on everything comes because they've learned how to make decisions as a couple.

As your marriage is in its infancy, the biggest change of all is growing accustomed to making decisions together. Where will we live? Where will we work? What channel will we watch tonight? Is it better to take a vacation or save the money for more Franklin Mint plates? And so on.

When you were single, these decisions were easy to make. You worked where you wanted to work. You lived where you wanted to live. And the channel stayed right where you put it last time you were watching TV. But there was something missing, wasn't there? You won every decision—it was you against yourself—but it was a hollow victory. So you decided to get married.

Now there are two parties in every decision. And you won't always agree. And that's no big deal. It takes some getting used to, and it takes a while to master the art of making decisions together, but it's one of the most important skills you'll develop as a couple.

Whether it's where to live or what channel to watch, practice making decisions as a couple. The skills you pick up making small decisions will help you when making big ones. Each of you have to consider three points of view: what you want, what your spouse wants, and what's best for you as a couple. Sometimes, what's best for both of you is something neither of you would have picked on your own.

Take the ridiculous example of "What channel shall we watch?" Maybe one of you wants to watch *World's Deadliest Police Animal Chases, Part III* and the other prefers Emma Thompson as Norton in *The Norton Anthology of Literature*. But since each of you is (rightfully) repelled at the other's choice, and you're going to spend the evening together, you make pick a third program, maybe *Casablanca*. One of you gives up the animal chases, the other gives up Emma, but when you're together, a World War II picture filled with intrigue and romance just feels right.

Now, that was an easy decision. And neither of you "won," but in some sense, both of you did. As you both consider the other's taste, values, and background in each decision, making mutually acceptable decisions becomes second nature. You learn what lines never to cross (she's allergic to snow peas; he won't eat any food that's blue) and which areas are open to compromise (she'll once in a while eat steak; he'll once in a while go square dancing). You learn to make little accommodations for your spouse—and for both of your sakes. And sooner or later you find that thinking as a couple comes as second nature. When you're making a decision that affects both of you, you automatically find yourself taking your partner's likes and dislikes into account before proposing something.

Even though it may sound like you're giving something up, oftentimes, to both partners' surprise, the "compromise" decision that neither of you would have picked by yourself works out better for both of you. Why that works out that way is anyone's guess.

Ways in Which Your Life Won't Change at All

Marriage is about the best thing that can happen to you, and yet . . . many people labor under unrealistic expectations of what their marriage might do for them. Here are a few ways in which life will remain the same:

- You won't get a raise at work.
- You won't get any better at fixing things around the house.

- You won't start eating more fruits and vegetables and fewer French fries.
- Your car won't stop making that clackety-clackety sound on cold days.
- You won't finish writing that screenplay.
- Your mom won't stop telling that embarrassing story about when you were a baby.
- You won't start liking opera any more than you do right now.
- Your acne won't clear up.
- You won't get over your fear of public speaking.
- You won't have much more insight into the meaning of it all than you do right now. The universe is mostly a mystery and it's going to stay that way.

That being said, you still found love.

Chapter 13

Everything You Absolutely Must Do Before Getting Married

lip and save.)

1. Obtain a valid marriage license in any of the 50 states (or another country). These are available during business hours at your county courthouse.
2. Fill out the license, sign it, date it, have your spouse-to-be sign and date it, have it properly witnessed, and then file the license with the proper authorities (e.g., the county clerk or marriage registrar).

You're married.

Chapter 14

Everything Else

AMERICAN STOCK PHOTOGRAPHY

$\mathcal{T}$he previous chapter is so short because a willing spouse, a witness, and a license properly filed are the only things you need to be legally married: *everything else is optional.*

This is not meant to belittle chauffeur-driven limousines or chamber orchestras or silk dresses or men and women of the cloth or people who sell preprinted thank-you cards imprinted with pictures of copyrighted Disney characters in wedding garb. Rather, understanding what is the absolute minimum to get married helps put the many things that make a wedding beautiful and memorable into perspective and helps you remember that they only *seem* obligatory. In fact, everything else is optional. Sometimes your wedding can feel like a mandatory class with arcane requirements imposed by the principal. It shouldn't. The two of you control this class, and you get to pick from a list of enticing options that you select. We're fortunate to live in an era and place where such lavish weddings are possible.

That said, most people want some pageantry. I did, my wife did, my parents did, my sisters did, my brother did. The only people I've ever seen do "the minimum" were in line at the county courthouse at the same time my wife and I got *our* license. The bride-to-be was also a mother-to-be and looked about nine and a half months' pregnant; one sneeze and she'd give birth before completely filling out all the forms. The husband-to-be looked very worried. They had the clerk read their vows for them.

And you know what? For $44, they wound up just as married as someone who spent $44,000. No doubt they would have preferred a big brass band and waiters in black tie, but they didn't *need* it. The rest of us are lucky enough to have weddings a little fancier. So here are the most popular options in a timetable so that you may plan them comfortably.

Six Months Before the Wedding (Or as Soon as You Get Engaged)
Set the date for your wedding
Make your first estimated budget
Choose a location for the ceremony
Choose a clergyperson or other officiant
Choose a location for the reception
Choose a location for the rehearsal dinner
Decide on the number of guests
Begin shopping for clothes:
> Wedding gown
> Formalwear for the groom
> Bridesmaids' dresses
> Groomsmen's clothes

Watch *It Happened One Night* on video

Between 3 and 6 Months Before the Wedding
Finalize guest lists and gather addresses
Choose your attendants:
> Maid or matron of honor
> Best man
> Bridesmaids
> Groomsmen
> Flower girl
> Ring bearer

Discuss and begin planning a honeymoon
Begin organizing a reception:

Finalize the location
Arrange for catering
Arrange for entertainment
Arrange for a photographer
Arrange for a videographer
Arrange for a florist
Finalize clothing choices
Register a gift list
Send announcements to newspapers
Order invitations and stationery
Watch *Four Weddings and a Funeral* on video

Between 2 and 3 Months Before the Wedding

Finish addressing invitations
Finalize honeymoon plans
Have a romantic dinner together without any discussion of
    the wedding whatsoever

Six Weeks Before the Wedding

Mail your invitations
Write thank-you notes as gifts begin to arrive
Make seating charts for:
    Rehearsal dinner
    Wedding
    Reception
Finalize plans and prices with vendors:
    Florist
    Caterer
    Music for ceremony
    Photographer
    Videographer
    Chauffeur
    Others: _____
Watch *The Wedding Singer* on video

Four Weeks Before the Wedding
Reconfirm all services
Order the wedding cake and groom's cake
Get your marriage license
Recontact invitees who haven't responded yet
Select gifts for bridesmaids, groomsmen
Test-fit any clothing to be purchased
Watch *Casablanca* on video

Two Weeks Before the Wedding
Pick up rings
Pick up gifts for bridesmaids, groomsmen
Finalize guest lists
Bachelor/bachelorette parties
Test-fit any rented clothing
Get great haircuts
Have a long, romantic walk

One Day Before the Wedding
Pick up all clothing
Rehearsal
Rehearsal dinner
Try to get a good night's sleep
No movie tonight: this is your life

The Big Day
Get married
Everything else is gravy

Chapter 15

The Last
24 Hours

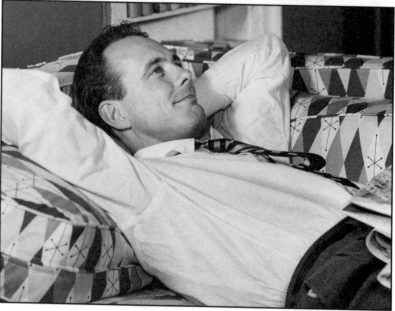

AMERICAN STOCK PHOTOGRAPHY

Part 1: Tomorrow, We Get Married

You've been planning for months or maybe even years, the vendors are hired, and the out-of-town guests are snugly stowed away in various houses, apartments, and hotels around the town where you'll get married.

You may feel like you did the night before your senior prom or your first day of school or the night before your birthday, but the night before your wedding is also different from all of those. Savor it.

The checklists, busywork, and obsession with details that accompanies any wedding can make you a little crazy, especially if the two of you are planning your own event. That's why you need to promise yourself that at a certain point you'll let go: forget about the Jordan almonds and just allow events to unfold. Pick a trusted delegate or two to handle any last-minute crises—good choices are the maid of honor or best man, or a parent or close friend—and leave instructions that after a certain time all problems go to them.

Now that the months of work are behind you, the time has come to enjoy the fruits of your labor. If the florist finds out that the airplane importing blue-green orchids from Caracas was blown off course by a hurricane, you don't need to know about it now. If the guy who crafts little teeny flowers out of icing breaks his hand in kung fu class, you don't need to know about that, either. People are surprisingly resourceful and capable of solving problems small and large when given the authority to do so.

The Rehearsal

Your rehearsal and rehearsal dinner will probably be held the night before your wedding. During your rehearsal, be sure to iron out any questions that have been making either of you feel anxious. Where do I stand? Where does my spouse-to-be stand? Who comes in first? Who leaves first?

If yours is a religious wedding, chances are the officiant has been through this many, many times. Ask every question that's bothering you. No matter how dumb you think your question may be, someone has undoubtedly asked it before. If you've had butterflies in your stomach or even nightmares about "what happens if something goes wrong," they'll go away once you stand in the actual place where the ceremony is going to take place, surrounded by the actual people who will be there on the big day. Reassuring, casual, and kind of fun, the rehearsal is a great shakedown cruise to remind you that getting married is actually kind of pleasant and fun. If the wedding you're planning is a big one, take a look at the place where you'll stage the ceremony while it's mostly empty. Try to remember what it looks like, because on the day of the wedding, you'll see only the faces of friends and loved ones.

The officiant takes charge of the rehearsal, and unlike the *real* ceremony, there's plenty of time to stop and do things over. Try to arrange for the musicians who will play at the wedding to also play at the rehearsal; the music cues the action, just like in a Broadway musical, and can help all parties involved choreograph their steps.

The Rehearsal Dinner

Following the strictest rules of etiquette, the rehearsal dinner is paid for by the groom and includes everyone who is officially in the wedding. "Official" members of the wedding include all the bridesmaids, groomsmen, maid or matron of honor, best man, parents, ushers, flower girls, ring bearers, and officiants. Be sure to invite the rabbi, priest, minister, or judge who is going to officiate, but don't be offended if he or she declines. Remember—you're doing this once, but the officiant may preside over scores of weddings every year. In addition to those "officially" invited to the rehearsal and rehearsal dinner, you may want to include out-of-town guests, particularly those who have traveled a long way. On the wedding day, there is often so much activity that neither of you will have much time to visit with far-flung friends; better to include them in the rehearsal dinner, where you have a little more time.

Rehearsal dinners are usually, but not always, less formal than the wedding. You may choose to hold it at the home of a friend or relative, or at a restaurant, or even have a picnic, depending on the time of year. Wherever you choose, be sure that the restaurant or host understands that you'll be lingering long after dinner. This is no time to "eat and run"; if you're at a restaurant, make arrangements ahead of time so that an employee can be on hand should you choose to stay after the closing time.

There's only one hard-and-fast rule about how to conduct yourself the night before your wedding: *No bachelor or bachelorette parties.* Some non–rocket scientist somewhere propagated the idea that the night before the wedding was the best time to have a knock-down, drag-out wild party with drinking, revelry, and debauchery. The aforementioned non–rocket scientist clearly did not take into account that the groom and bride who pursued such a course of action on their last night before getting married would be in pretty sorry shape on the wedding day itself. However, the legend that the wedding eve is for partying persists, perhaps popularized by fine motion pictures like that classic for the ages, *Bachelor Party,* and the masterpiece tour de force of modern cinema, *Bachelor Party II.* If that's how you wish to spend the last night before getting married, rent the movies; don't reenact them.

$\mathcal{D}$o not throw a bachelor (or bachelorette) party the night before your wedding.

AMERICAN STOCK PHOTOGRAPHY

After the Rehearsal Dinner

At some point, the rehearsal dinner will be over, you'll wish everyone good night, and all will go their separate ways. Even if the two of you already live together, you may wish to stay in separate homes for this one night. Kiss each other good night and know that the next time you'll see each other will be on the wedding day itself.

A romantic tradition that's worth perpetuating is a night-before-the-wedding care package. The groom prepares one for the bride and the bride prepares one for the groom. The care package isn't to be opened until you're apart from each other, and it isn't fancy. It should include a childhood photo that your spouse-to-be has never seen before, a short letter, and a small surprise. What kind of surprise? I'm not telling, because anything published in a book won't be much of a surprise, will it? Think small, think personal, think, "the kind of thing that only my spouse-to-be will understand." One bride-to-be included her fiancé's favorite candy bar; a groom put a tape recorder and a special mix tape of songs for his fiancée to listen to on the night before their wedding.

After you've gone your separate ways on the wedding eve, try to keep the phone calls short and sweet and try to get some sleep. You've got a big day ahead of you.

Part 2: The Day of the Wedding

By now, each of your respective fates should be in the hands of a trusted friend: for the bride, the maid (or matron) of honor, and for the groom, the best man. Make them earn their titles. Don't be surprised if you're feeling dreamy or distracted on your wedding day; everyone is. Don't be flustered by unimportant things. By the time that you get this far, there's nothing that can be done about any of the vendors or any travel arrangements. You have a more important job to do today—you're getting married.

In a traditional ceremony, bridesmaids wear matching outfits.

AMERICAN STOCK PHOTOGRAPHY

Pack Ahead

A few days before the wedding, each of you should pack the things you'll need for the wedding day itself into a small suitcase. Keep it separate from the bags you plan to take on the honeymoon; this is just for the day itself. Pack the clothes you'll need. For the bride, that includes one change of clothes to wear before putting on The Dress with a capital D, The Dress and its accessories, and a change of clothes for after the wedding. Similarly, the groom will need three changes of clothing, though we hope he won't be packing a dress.

Each of you packs an "emergency" kit, mainly to set your minds at ease so that the morning of the wedding you won't panic that you forgot something. Pick a small suitcase or bag and leave it open in your home for a week or so before the wedding. Every time you experience a moment of panic— *"What if on my wedding day I forget* _____(fill in the blank)—simply throw the item in question into the bag. This could include extra changes of underwear, grooming supplies, makeup for her, photocopies of any religious writings or poems that you intend to read at the wedding, bottled water, gum, or anything else that you might need.

Stage Fright

Public speaking always heads the list of popular phobias. More people are more afraid of speaking in public than are afraid of snakes, lizards, aliens, and killer tornadoes combined. Sometimes, someone suffering "wedding jitters" is simply suffering from stage fright. Simply understanding that your fear relates to public speaking and not to the wedding per se is a giant step toward addressing the problem. Equally fortunate is that there are a variety of strategies to grapple with stage fright:

• Remember that you're surrounded by friends. One at a time, none of these people would pose the tiniest threat. Even in groups of 5 or 10, you wouldn't be self-conscious for a second.

• Understand that a little bit of stage fright can be helpful. You shouldn't saunter down the aisle like you're shopping at Wal-Mart. A small amount of nervous energy will serve you well.

• If, before walking down the aisle, you're still nervous, try a breathing exercise. Sit down and close your eyes. Inhale slowly through your nose, then exhale slowly through your mouth. Repeat this a few times. If you fall asleep, you've relaxed too much.

• Remember that the business end of the ceremony is in the hands of the officiant. If you listen carefully and follow directions, you'll be fine. There may seem to be long pauses, but from the point of view of those watching, it all goes by incredibly fast.

The day of the wedding, *nothing can go wrong, as long as at the end of the day you're married to each other.* To set your mind at ease, reflect in advance about what might happen when something goes awry. *What if . . .*

• *. . . One of you says the wrong thing during the ceremony?* The officiant will correct you, and you'll say it again.

• *. . . One of you is late to the ceremony?* Then everyone will wait. This isn't the second grade. No one is going to mark you tardy.

• *. . . Someone in the bridal party doesn't show up?* You weigh his or her absence against your discomfort, and when you feel you've waited an appropriate amount of time, you proceed apace. Of course, you'd wait longer for the father of the bride than for someone sitting in the last row, but if people are late, it's their loss, not yours.

$\mathscr{N}$o matter what goes wrong, the important thing is to be married at the end of the day.

AMERICAN STOCK PHOTOGRAPHY

- *. . . The outdoor ceremony is rained out?* First, go inside. Then, get married. Rain on a wedding day is lucky. (Alanis Morissette says it's "ironic," but she doesn't know the meaning of the word *ironic*. Look it up in the dictionary if you doubt her error.) After the indoor ceremony is over, everyone can talk about El Niño and global warming.
- *. . . A car breaks down?* Get a ride.
- *. . . A seam splits?* Sew it up.
- *. . . There's not enough room for everyone who was invited to sit down?* Consider yourselves well loved and very lucky to have so many people who want to wish you well.
- *. . . What if, what if, what if?* The list of worries can extend for hours. Write them down, if it makes you feel better. You probably will have a few minor screwups, you probably won't have any major catastrophes, and for each potential mishap there's a simple and easy solution.

Don't Miss Your Own Wedding

Some people have the perfect clothes, a beautiful bridal party, handsome groomsmen, a reception worthy of the Ritz, and a honeymoon in paradise, and yet they still manage to miss their own wedding. Ask them afterward how it was and all they'll talk about are the vendors and the guests and the splendor, and if you ask how they felt during the whole affair, they might say, "Thank God it's over."

Don't let this happen to you.

Make the wedding day *your* day. Appreciate all the details; look into the faces of those who have come to witness your union. Stop and smell the flowers—literally. Listen to the music; feel the special texture of the clothing against your skin. These aren't everyday clothes, and this isn't an everyday event. No matter how many people are photographing and videotaping the big wedding day, no medium yet devised can record your feelings as the event is unfolding. Don't wait for the photos to come back to find out how you felt.

Think about the everyday meaning of the words that you say during the wedding ceremony. "Vows" are just solemn promises. The officiant may have repeated them a thousand times before, you may have practiced saying them, but when you say them today, think about what they mean; and when your spouse-in-the-making is speaking, listen carefully. Whether yours are the traditional vows you've heard before or a unique ceremony created especially for this occasion, this is the only time they really count. And after the ceremony, you're no longer fiancé and fiancée. You'll be husband and wife.

Welcome to the best part of your life.

AMERICAN STOCK PHOTOGRAPHY